FALL, WINTER AND SPRING

FALL, WINTER AND SPRING

A Poetry Collection

By

Todd French

ReadersMagnet, LLC

FALL

FIRST CRUSH/AUTUMN THOUGHTS

When you are on your sickbed, when you are failing fast,
What will you see when Memory's relentless oyster shucker
Flicks his blade open and starts rooting for pearls-white or black,
Prying at the hasps of shell, exposing them-nacre's milk/bonefire
To the blazing orange and red filigree of life/your *life's*
Tangelo sunset

Will you see-will it all come into numbing clarity like stars framed in
The lens of a Celestron Powerseeker

The day
That day

When you were a boy with a balsa glider in your hand and one
Afternoon rounded the corner and there she was, sitting on her
Front porch, tying the laces of her first pair of roller skates,
The cuts and abraded skin of her knees drawing your attention
Before you looked up into her face as she looked up, parting the screen
Of her long honey-blonde hair dusted with day-flecks of bright carnelian,
And she fixed you with her bright and beautiful moth-green eyes,
A mixture of playfulness and gravity there beyond your experience,
And each detail-the cunningly snubbed nose, the wide and
Vulnerable forehead, the bottom lips slightly fuller than the upper
And the bridge of the nose dusted with a seme of freckles,
The whole of *her* seemed capable of flinging you through an eternity
Of roadside billboards like you were in a Chuck Jones cartoon

And you felt like Bellerophon bucked off Pegasus when the hero
Was halfway to heaven

Do you remember how it all bore down on you like the
Biggest yellow Volkswagen bug tearing out of the golden west
And the rest upended-baseball and baseball cards, monster mags,
Aurora and Tamiya plastic models, bike patrols, football with
Dad, backyard forts, treehouse gang meets, vacant houses and
Dares, movies, carob tree pod fights

And when she said "Hi," in a voice soft as a winter marten's fur,
And you, gob-smacked and flummoxed, managed to respond.
Could you have floated the balsa glider to her, mouthing the words

This
And
Me
I
Think.

Will you remember the first face that upthrust you past your
Callow understanding like a gladiator's trident into a world of light
And notion un-thought and un-felt?

DICTATORS AND REVENANTS

I know that Putin is a dictator and so is Zelensky:
I know that the latter has outlawed opposition parties,
Persecuted the Russian Orthodox Church in the Ukraine,
That he regulates the news media and just as Putin
Has employed the brutal Wagner Group, so Zelensky fields
The far-right Azov regiment-with its runic badge.
And yes, I know this-and do not excuse-this man or his regime
For the threats to suspend elections if he doesn't get more of
Our money, and the allegations involving the infuriating,
Dirty Burisma Holdings Limited malfeasance involving our
President Biden and his troubled son Hunter. No bones about it:
It all stinks, ugly as stump water,a nuked atoll's crater sand, numbing
To the mind: painful, endlessly agonizing as if you reached into
The garage's dark to steady yourself and thrust your hand through
The web of a black widow spider, then the web of a
Sydney funnel-web beneath that, and through that, a recluse,
And then a redback and at last a banana spider and so on-toxic bite
After toxic bite-that's how it feels these days-and with
No end that we can see to the blood, loss, sorrow and grief.

I know all this.

But here we are in autumn-a time for mortal intimations,
Insights sharp and chilling as the cold, canted rutilant light
Of the short days hovers in the wings. It is a time when
The intellect peruses the sheaves, the hayricks of
Forbidding connections under the cold-rind of a blade-thin

Sickle moon; it marks the semaphore of star-shine on
The scarecrow's button eyes-the flash of an ax-head
Leaning against the serrated cut-out of a twisted oak.
It speaks in the sibilance of grain's scrape and night breeze
In the ears and soul-it hoots like a barn owl in the back acre.
And we take stock-in the October rows and furrows, in the
Wheat stacks of all we have done that year-and we sort through
Uneasy dreams of lingering shades-ghosts and revenants because
Autumn is a time when white faces flash between the dark boles:
Skeletal Ventian *bautus, columbinas, morettas* and *voltos*
Conjured out of cold helixes of dead leaf, twig and wind.
Old loves, dead loves, old friends, old focs gone on-those with whom
We fell out of touch-and so we go through old photo

Albums, half-forgotten letters, yearbooks and keepsakes.
You count the aches, agues, crowsfeet, the hairline's recession,
The gray and the threads of white in your wife's sable tresses,
The cold breeze in the house that you cannot isolate and eliminate,
But you can feel its passage as you go from room to room;
The wind-fumble and leaf-scrabble at the window screens,
The white in the dog's muzzle and flicker of the porch's amber bulb,
The little winks and nudges from the Boney King of Nowhere.
It is the season, gusty and grim for examining losses and scales,
The drifting chaff and straw fall of discontentments and peeves,
Regrets sifted by the remorseless winnowing fan-for the
Retrieval of windfalls from a scraggly, picked-through orchard.
On the heels of that understanding, comes this realization,
That in spite of all the terrible things uncovered regarding
This interminable war between Russia and the Ukraine,

I remember *her*.

I will not forget *her* though stroke or embolism fell me,
My heart fail as I am reaching for a cup of coffee in the kitchen
Or while I am on my deathbed expiring of a terrible disease.

I see

The Ukrainian girl, dressed in her voluminous prom gown,
Bespeaking defiance, celebrating her class Graduation Waltz
Amidst the heaped rubble piles of her bombed-out school;
Her dress the deep scarlet of a matador's *muleta* cloak,
The shade of anger, defiance, No Quarter-paint the decks red,
The deep red of blood's/life's hope-she stood there, coiffed and
Solemn, eyed downcast, flanked by blasted brick and buckled pipes,
As if to simply say *I am alive, I am still alive and I believe*
I have a future-my nation has a future-though blood and fire,
Though gun, missile, mortar, tank and 'copter tell me otherwise,
I will live and enter the world of experience and labor,
I will love and have a life-and this, this will end, God let it end.
She stands there-demoiselle unbowed by war's detritus,
Red as a cardinal or summer tanager singing its song of life
Even in the face of a forest's conflagration. There she is:
The specter in the photos memorializing her youth before
The merciless gaze of the *bogatyrs* and *kyrs* of brute, negative might.

I do not know if she is still alive (but she has graduated)
Of if she is another ghost joining the others of this generation
Haunting the ruins of her old school or some other mead of misery
In her country.

But

I will never forget the red rose
Hanging on to one last petal
Beneath the unremitting salvos
Of spring's hard hail

MIA KHALIFA SAYS FLIP THE PHONES

"Can someone please tell the freedom fighters in Palestine to flip their phones and
film horizontal," Mia Khalifa

That we were Polyphemus blinded by Odysseus' fire-hardened spear,
Or, that we could burrow underground in a licorice-black moil of
Carapace and mandible-be heavy-lidded toads pulsing like hearts
Beneath garden stonse-then see this, see this, these horrors vivid as
The day-glo daubs on toxic salamanders-how can we believe what we see,
How can we conceive of the savagery, unspeakable hate and atavism
Married to today's tech-minotaurs and Rephaims messing with their Apples,
The terrorists filming the young girl, her clothes in shreds, careening
About the back of their jeep-the dismembered bodies of IDF soldiers, babies,
Oh God babies in chicken-cages, mocked by their captors, how can this be?
Mia Khalifa, the porn star asked the Hamas killers to flip their phones
And film horizontally-she was irked by their ineptitude they showed in properly
Catching the aesthetics of atrocity, rape, murder, torture and massacre
(Hamas is threatening to release films of the hostage on this day of Rage).
She wanted a better viewing experience-and the Yale professor stated that
Settlers aren't civilians-are we sleepers walking through a *grand guignol*,
A cold rehearsal for Jacobean blood squibs-dreamers simply passing
Other somnambulists entraining our nightmares as they jingle their
Chainmail butchers' aprons, their eyes wide as a flying foxes
Weaving through the cold enamel of the corridors of the subconscious?
How can anyone glory in this, how can anyone cheer the slaughter on?
There is something-there is something-that is not The Lamb in you;
There is something-a verdigris of the soul-that has nothing of The Lamb
In you.

*("Can someone please tell the freedom fighters in Palestine to flip their phones and film
horizontal")*

Surely Hell profited from some happenstance-accident of warp and weft of
Space/Time/Wormhole and the bad angels that forsook their first estate
Received a month's furlough to harrow this bloody breadth of earth?
Did some *Nephilim* with ash-black pinions and bleeding goat's eyes produce
A parole loophole from some half-forgotten bit of nether-scroll?
If only we could blame this on a prison-break of motivated devils:
That somehow, Michael and Gabriel fell asleep at the wheel.
How can human beings behead babies in their cribs?
Here is the bloodied teenage girl being herded into the Hamas vehicle.
Here are children forced to watch their parents gunned down.
Here are parents forced to watch their children gunned down.
Here is the wheelchair-bound Holocaust survivor kidnapped by Hamas.
Here are our streets overflowing with terror's apologists.
Here are crowds shouting Gas the Jews in Sydney, Australia.
Here are students at Harvard demonstrating-stumping for Hamas.
Here is the congresswoman fleeing the reporter asking her to condemn
These atrocities-still flying the Palestinian flag outside her office.
Here is the View woman comparing Hamas to The Proud Boys.
Here is our President stumbling like a mummy on a half-ration of
Tannis leaves: when will he ask for the flags to be flown at half-mast?
The mind reels: let us help up on Rhodes' beach, a centurion's cloak
Of scarlet on our shoulders while we stumble up the goat paths,
The black sky coughing lightning tines-rain and sleet in our faces.

("can someone please tell the freedom fighters-")

Let us stand and be appalled by the dancers at The Werewolf Ball.
The mind is appalled by the steps assayed at The Werewolf Ball.

(--"to flip their phones and film horizontal?")

Do you wonder that God will darken the sun for a third of the day?
Do you wonder that some hearts are darkened the entire day?
Mia Khalifa asked the Hamas terrorists to flip their phones and
Film horizontal.

RIVER LETHE

In <u>Greek mythology</u>, **Lethe** (/ˈliːθiː/; <u>Ancient Greek</u>: Λήθη *Léthē*; <u>Ancient Greek</u>: [lɛ́ːtʰɛː], Modern Greek: [ˈliθi]), also referred to as **Lesmosyne**, was one of the five rivers of the underworld of <u>Hades</u>. Also known as the *Amelēs potamos* (river of unmindfulness), the Lethe flowed around the cave of <u>Hypnos</u> and through the Underworld where all those who drank from it experienced complete forgetfulness. Lethe was also the name of the Greek spirit of forgetfulness and oblivion, with whom the river was often identified.

In Classical Greek, the word *lethe* (λήθη) literally means "oblivion", "forgetfulness", or "concealment".[1] It is related to the Greek word for «truth», *aletheia* (<u>ἀλήθεια</u>), which through the <u>privative alpha</u> literally means «un-forgetfulness» or «un-concealment».

An <u>Orphic inscription</u>, said to be dated from between the second and third century B.C. warns readers to avoid the Lethe and to seek the <u>Mnemosyne</u> instead. Drinkers of the Lethe›s water would not be quenched of their thirst, often causing them to drink more than necessary.[2] (Wikipedia)

And there they were-young and passionate-raging outside the universities with
Their Palestinian flags-the new stumblers, bumblers in the warrens of Hades,
The hasty bibbers of Lethe's unmindful waters, chivvied to its banks by
Dishonest, hateful teachers. *These are our sons and daughters*, I thought,
These coma-consciences carried down Hypnos' cave, sonic pings of bat screams
And blind roach's chitin for their guides-they didn't see the slain babies,
The butchered families, the Hamas terrorists posing with fearful children,
The paragliders descending like furies on the concert-goers, or driving
The bruised and bloodied teen girl to slavery and rape. Somewhere, in between
Draughts of amnesia (this is where the dead drank to forget their former lives),
(and the living should never drink from the waters of Umindfulness)

They had dreamt/swilled away the death's-head cap, the camps, crematoriums,
The living skeletons standing behind barbed wire, the mass graves,
The belching chimneys, the delousing lines overseen by beer-breathed sergeants
And liquor-addled Kapos, the box-cars, piles of suitcases mounds of
Gold fillings and eyeglasses and yet here they were: praising massacre,
Blessing atrocities-showing solidarity for the unspeakable, for pure evil.
These were our sons and daughters, forgetful of the past and quick to
Cherish what was indefensible, fight for what was vile. What had they
Been taught-what wine of Cthonic Zeus had they guzzled that they could
Be so blind, that they could forget Never Again and the Nuremberg trials?

How was this possible?
How could anyone forget?
How could anyone forget Hitler, Himmler, Heydrich, Frank, Hoss, Eichmann,

The Bony King of Air-Masticators and his crow-black condottiere?

Our sons and daughters: who set your feet on the road to forgetfulness?

In the sunless land, who drew your syllabus up, beside the moles and voles,
And bone-colored buttercup?

How could this generation forget the Holocaust and insist the beheading
Of babies and execution of whole families was reciprocity, normal rules of
Engagement-tit for tat? Standing there, under the outspread cypress
Shadowing Hades' palace and waterway-how could we not see you
Quaffing the stream-vino of thought-blotto-obliteration of anamnesis:
When you knelt down amidst the pale grass of the twilit-dusted bank to
Scoop up the next mouthful, did the ghosts in their translucent greaves and
Brush-topped helmets, flesh left in gobbets and tatters on some crimson field,
Turn to you (interlopers dead in decency but not life) as they made room and
Say: "Don't look at the fish as they rise up-don't make eye-contact, lest
You remember-lest you recall. Just fill your palms and do not refrain. I have
Forgotten my best girl in Troy-all but the arch of her columnar neck-now no
More than a few broken bricks of ivory-one sea-green eye rubbed out of
The sparking strand of unraveled memory." And did a peddler, as
Insubstantial and luminous as filaments of moon-speckled webs' skeins, say:
"I have nearly forgotten the starving children I left in Corinth: a few more

　　　　　　　　　　TODD FRENCH

Sips and their bones and hollows will intrude no more-their cries but
Bee buzz at dusk."

I wonder if our children, as they drank from the amphora of
Academia's criminal neglect and lies, fingers fisting about their flags and placards,
Denying the reality of horrors and responsibility going against the grain
Of indoctrination
muttered in sleepy confusion:

I think I have forgotten a test I should have taken or failed a test I should
Have passed

There is a test I should have passed.

What was the test I should have passed?

And we, looking on in horror, aping Orpheus with his lyre, leaning against the
Poplar where the Mnemosyne, the Pool of Memory shimmers in the drab
And drifting half-dusk, reply:
Yes, there was a test and you utterly failed. For the sake of your souls, drink
From the Mnemosyne while there is time while there is hope.

AUTUMN RAINS/10/01/23

And Just like that, the reefs of cloud, the thick gray of lynx fur
Sweep in, the flat light of autumn piercing the sky's overlay
Rendering the red flowers of the crape myrtles on Slater
The dull half-smudged red of old pomegranates. The heart brims
Even as the joints and muscles ache when we watch the
Heavens' denim blue overwhelmed and the first gusts
Make the backyard chimes shiver, tinkle and gong, cause
The owl scarecrows in our neighbor's yard pitch and yaw
On their mounts like a ship's mast in a gale, while our own
Crow scarecrow (a crow decoy hanging upside down by its feet),
Pendulums back and forth from the limb rope of a Japanese privet
Like the charred remains of a damned soul hanging by its
Heels over the pit. The green everywhere whickers while
Every palm is turned into a span of accordion pleat.
And the leaves quiver, detach and spin-kicked along in
Anhydrous phalanxes across the spavined lawns and concrete.
The temperature drops. The flags on the block flap like
Laundry on a line and their metal holders creak and ping.
The wind flips our collar, scarves ripple and twist like congers,
And loose shirt-tails flare like the ends of fork-tailed flycatchers.
And like that, we are reacquainting ourselves with the birth of
The Dying Time, as if we were running our fingers through
Lazarus' cast off shroud as it slips from his ambulatory form.

And best of all

And best of all-best of all, the smell of ozone,

The smell of ozone-welcome as an old friend's phone call
Impinges right before the first sprinkles fall, darkening brick
And concrete, turning the foliage slick and shiny.

It doesn't last long: the clouds move on and the sun's rowel
Rips rents in the overcast, releasing a brace of dishwater-colored
Beams and rays-the bright working over our eyes.
But it doesn't matter because the season, with its gunmetal
Proscenium and first, tentative drizzles already has us dreaming awake
Of rain drumming on the roof, loud as stadium applause,
While we scoot to find the right fold in the couch, steaming mug
In hand, a good book on the table or disk ON PAUSE,
The heater imparting warmth through the house thick as caramel.
We consider the rain-snakes sliding down the fogged glass,
The louvres in the kitchen cracked so-in between storm
Salvos-we can catch the occasional strains from a dogged,
Bedraggled sparrow, lazuli bunting or black phoebe,
Weary but insistent as a good cop trying to talk a hurt girl
Off a building ledge-or some believing soul pulling off a
Pure and merciful deed, pinning it to the crow and grackle
Black calendar squares of life in War-Time. The warmth inside,
The cold outside

Bespeaks the season like taking a whiff from a shelled walnut.

But really

It's just so nice to hear/feel/smell
The autumn rains
Again.

FATHERS AND DAUGHTERS

"They just said, 'We found Emily, she's dead,' and I went, 'Yes,'" he said.
"I went 'Yes,' and smiled because that is the best news of the possibilities
That I knew. The best possibility that I was hoping for," he said.

Thomas Hand on hearing of the death of his daughter Emily
At the hands of Hamas terrorists

I came across the story of the Irishman in Israel who discovered
That his young daughter had been murdered by Hamas terrorists:
She had been spared being taken hostage and subjected to a fate
Worse than death-and he was thankful. He was thankful she was dead,
Not subjected to rape and slavery by Stone Age Morlocks, by *things*,
Blind to decency, shorn of humanity and I, a father with three girls,
Mind freighted with colliding horrors like a cargo-ship's burden
On a storm-hammered sea, thought about those words that no father,
No mother, that no parent should ever have to frame into words,
Should never be forced to entertain in a civilized society where
Noncombatants-women and children, the old and infirm-should
Never come to harm. Those few lines, uttered by Mr. Hand,
Who would bear years of no more than the ghosts of his Emily's smiles,
Continued to reverberate in my thoughts-like the sad glissandos
And howls of dogs during dishwater days of Earthquake Weather:

"They just said, 'We found Emily, she's dead,' and I went, 'Yes,'" he said.
"I went 'Yes,' and smiled because that is the best news of the possibilities
That I knew. The best possibility that I was hoping for," he said.

How does a life become no more than a photograph in a frame
On the mantle-a dozen or so crayoned pictures on the wall,
A ceramic cup with Happy Birthday, Daddy scribed on the side
Underneath a smiling sun?

I read the words and went outside and stood a while in the
Unseasonable brightness and heat, and considered those short,
Heartbreaking sentences as my own girls bustled about their chores
Inside and thought of the atrocities that befall families with the ease
Of a leopard dropping down from his sleeping tree or a swan
Lighting down on a morning lake's pellucid mirror. I thought about
The father who had left Ireland thirty years before and come to Be'eri
As a volunteer-planning only to stay a few months-but remained.
His little girl (who had lost her mother to cancer) had been at a
Sleepover with friends in Kibbutz Be'eri when the terrorists struck.
How could anyone drop their child off at a sleepover and imagine
There would be no morning reunion-the little one breathlessly
Telling Dad what she and her friends did, what they watched,
What they ate, the jokes, the nano-second fall-outs and forgiveness,
How could a father-or any parent-conceive that there would be
No more mornings, just Endless Night, and recovery-following
A flashlight's dying beam across leagues of starless sand and
Joshua tree.

I lingered outside in the midday sunshine and watched the un-haunted
World of nature go about its green, God-given biz: the honeybees
Going from chrysanthemum to daisies while yellow sulfurs and
Fire-skippers flitted through the lantana-and yellow-bellied warblers
And green finches shot past quick as arbalest bolts, and the sun's
Golden rowel gouged its way across the robin blue sky without pause:
It couldn't stick to the sky for a day-as it did for Joshua-in outrage
Over the unspeakable because little girls had been massacred,
Babies beheaded, someone's daughter (living) hauled away by
Pre-civilizational savages to be held hostage-or raped and murdered.
I thought of an infinite number of daughters in an infinite number
Of trucks and jeeps (and my own girls) flying past Kibbutz rubble
Toward cheerless desert-and I considered the day that went on its

Merry way-because in spite of the pagans who extoll it-Nature is
Oblivious, without conscience or cognizance, and blooms and ewes
Come into being whatever monstrosities are mulled over in the minds
Of men and women-like Neanderthals sketching their battle-plans
In cave dirt-the sun shines, zephyrs and waves swell, fruit ripens,
And dogs snap at butterflies and birds sing. The green world
Continues spinning on its axis, and increments of sun, warmth,
Volition-the seamless dreams of beluga whales and crows go on.

And I thought of an infinite, perpetually grieving God in His heaven,
Holding a head vaster than the biggest gas giant, His brain bearing
Horrors past, present, future, multiplied into infinity-each and every
Moment-dreamt and executed, refined and improved by His creation.
I thought of Him in the Third Heaven sorrowing over His children,
And I grappled with His pain, as the Father of a Son, whom He could not
Whisk away from Gethsemane's garden any more than the bereaved
Father in Israel could save his daughter and her friends and
Their mother from the bullets and knives of the human monsters who
Mowed them down. I tried to imagine the suffering of a supreme being,
The tears shed for the First Rebellion on heaven's golden streets,
One-third of the angels whom He loved-serving lights snuffed out,
To the Last Rebellion in the Valley of Jehoshaphat, when, finally,
The notions of warring nations, racism, ethnic hates, identities and borders
Would be rendered moot-and I reflected on The Father who knew
What it was like to lose His Son-His boy, to murderous brutes,
Their hearts cold as star-fields, empty as tundra-and to not be
Able to intervene-but shut His eyes when the request for the cup's pass
Came to His ears-to turn away when that Son took on the weight of Sin
There on the cross.

And He, the grieving God in His heaven,
Holding a head vaster than the biggest gas giant, His brain bearing
Horrors past, present, future, multiplied into infinity-each and every
Moment-dreamt and executed, allowing Evil Men whom we blush
To call Men, to go about their butcheries and abominations
(until He mows them down like the green herb),
Knowing what it's like to lose a child, to watch His child,

   TODD FRENCH

And everyone's child who dies by violence from start to finish,
World Without End, Universe Without End.

(I knew you before you before I formed you in the womb)

I thought of Mr. Hand, the father who
Blessed the (less for him) unthinkable when it happened
In the freshness of his grief-to reporters

And I imagined that God saying, if He was interviewed in the
First moments of His grief:

"I thank Myself that My Son saved them-because that is the best news
Of the possibilities that I knew. That was the best possibility
That I was hoping for I thank God my Son can save them."

AUTUMN 2023

I am still looking forward to it, even though it starts
With the cold breeze that hits every nook and corner of the
House like a frisky ferret or stoat off the leash, and even
The cups of tea, lattes (don't say pumpkin spice), cider
Fail to banish its attack on your joints and bones. The
Extra blankets, afghans and coverlets come out of the
Cabinet and your old retriever or beagle continues to
Worry away at the one that's *his or hers and no others.*
Cats find their comfortable and inconvenient spot in
The hallway near the heater. Summer done-done in, packs
In its draggy heliotrope and magnolia mornings as the
Sky turns into an inverted bowl of frosted porcelain glass,
While the brittle leaves of elm, maple, sugar gum and prunus
Execute cartwheels and donuts on the drab, flat-lined lawns,
When the wind goes from a chilly, fitful riffle at the neck
To solid gusts. The park vistas turn into gun-oil still-lifes,
Of stripped deciduous trees festooned with brush smears
Of crazy-eyed Grackles and querulous crows.

Everyone

Moves against the wind and hammer-whack of leafage
Reduced to papyrus dry. Nature prunes its deadwood
And woodsmoke rises from chimneys. The storm gull
Heavens and roving winds and stropping-belt sharpened
Breezes make the plaintive cries of the puppies down the block
A little bit more lost and sometimes, as the world goes

Monochrome you find yourself thinking of a face and name
In an old photo album, or searching on-line for someone
You dated in school or the Google photos of your old
Family home in Compton or Lynwood-the season squeezes
Out-with its pall and deathlights-memories cast in amber,
Long walks where you take stock. After dinner, you find
Yourself paging through profiles on Facebook, trying to
Remember the names of ghosts and revenants.

What was their name again?
Where did they go?
Whom did they marry?
Are they still alive?

That's on the cold days-the North Sea world swell days.
But then there's the late afternoons when the huge
Flayed ball of the sun, the molten hue of factory slag,
Goes down, its rays casting patches of scarlet and gold
Across the bark of the block trees, bright as Mycenae funerary masks,
And tipping the wind-fluttered leaves with stuttering light
Like neon tubes on the brink of going out. You stand on the
Withered grass and take it in-the half-sun's blood arc sheeting the
Rooftops with its radiance and you catch the movement of
A hummingbird darting amidst the red-purple tendrils of
Bougainvillea on their wall, the flowers the reddish purple
Of a Byzantine emperor's buskins or the old dye of long-dead Tyre,
And as you catch

The blizzard squall of falling pink-white prunus blossoms, to be
Breeze-whipped across sidewalk and road it hits you

That this is autumn/cider/pumpkin/hayrick/Jack/scarecrow
Canning jar (do women still can or is that patriarchal oppression)
Wind-chime/early bike light/low night mist and morning fog
Thanksgiving/Halloween/apples and pears in the bowl and
Artichokes beets broccoli cauliflower and lettuce in the crisper

The realization comes with the start of cricket chirp and tremolo
Warbler and sparrow song loosed by the last of day's blood-blossom
On the horizon-the tangelo fusion of orange and crimson mixed
With peach fading into the light defuse blue of dark

The realization comes with the quiet drop of an abandoned
Wasp nest from its place beneath the eaves

Autumn.

Autumn-yes, autumn is here.

SONG/09/25/23

Give God the praise: let the words go forth like blood bays,
Pintos, paint horses, Appaloosas and blazers from the paddock;
Let thanksgiving rush from your soul like a storm of thoroughbreds
Released when the sun begins its golden enfilade against the earth.
Send forth an *Ascent* as sweet as the kinnor of King David,
The fruit of the lips as you drive to work, or silently, within.
May thanksgiving speed like a horse-herd in the tangelo dawn;
Like the sheep-in the gray North Sea breakers-coming down a
Mountain road in sunset's wane of scarlet light and indigo cloud.
Is it not Monday and has He not given us the hope of employment?

The golden bowl is intact and the silver cord has not been cut.

Here is morning's blazon on the kitchen table-here is the
Tortoiseshell with periscope tail rubbing against your legs.
The footfalls of the children are pounding back and forth upstairs;
Your wife or husband is getting the coffee underway.
It is good to have *volition* and *motion*; it is good to have
Meaning to scribe over the palimpsest of the week.

Give the Lord gratitude for the work of your hands,
Whether you will be arguing before a jury for justice,
Traveling the roads of a far state with your welder's rig,
Helping a trauma patient through their pain in a bad city's ward,
Or meeting your month's quota of car sales-thank God for
The start of the week with the surety of *Use*!
As the bee sings its secret, muzzy *Aubades* and *Virelais* to the roses

And hydrangeas in the first light of morn-as the golden oriole
Descants from the elm-pay Him good words for the work you will
Accomplish by the sweat of your brow, for the dollars and coins
He gives you to live.

It is good to receive work from the Lord.
It is fair to receive employment from His hand.

It is a blessing to fill our children's bellies with bread.

PRESIDENT JOE BIDEN OF AMERICA/ AUTUMN DREAMS 2023

Two gates the silent house of Sleep adorn;
Of polish'd ivory this, that of transparent horn:
True visions thro' transparent horn arise;
Thro' polish'd ivory pass deluding lies.
Of various things discoursing as he pass'd,
Anchises hither bends his steps at last.
Then, thro' the gate of iv'ry, he dismiss'd
His valiant offspring and divining guest.[9]

The Aeneid, Virgil

Socrates: "Listen then," I said, "to my dream, to see whether it comes through horn or through ivory."[5]

Charmides, Plato

I think you are no more than a shoe-stop in between ivory's door
And frame, and the chthonic liars, the spirits of Untruth, the Manes,
Pass your haunted mind back and forth as if it were no more substantial
Than an old badminton shuttlecock, light as mussel chips or the
Aragonite of dead coral. And it seems to me you are as ghost, a
Mylar balloon blown to bursting with sour helium of lies, deceptions,
Misremembered visions. There is no Cumaean Sibyl to accompany
You, as she did the son of Aphrodite, the hero fated to set Troy's sons
Firmly in their new home of Latium. The things he saw! He spied

Age, Fear and Hunger (do you dream those for us?), as well as monsters,
Unforgiving Dido and the future greatness of Rome. What do you see,
Prisoner of Ivory's forbidding entry, you who touted Build Back Better
As the promise for this land, for this America? You are webbed in
The turnstile of tenebrous mendacities, as the clouded drab or Quaker
Moth in the spider's threads. You have dreamt us calamities and
Disasters and there is no extricating you. How do the Manes appear to
You: as your satyr-brained son, naked, a hash-pipe in his mouth,
Riding the back of the Chimaera, an easel and brush-bag on his shoulder?
Do you see Putin, carried in the arms of the hapless giant Tityos, he of
The purloined liver, the prey of vultures? Does Xi rush by you, bearing
Khamenei on his shoulders, as Aeneas bore his father Anchises when
The holy towers of Ilium fell?

You have lost the stars of the asphodels-the torches that might have led you
From the underworld, that would have passed you through the gate of horn.

There is no hope of your return.

DOGS AND TUNNELS

It was both satisfying and horrifying: this was justice-the Israeli
Military dog caught in the rain-gray cone of light from the
Camera on its back-back fur and head in close-up hurtling forward
Through the Hamas terrorist tunnel-the soldier close behind, the
Wan light cutting through the cramped stygian darkness
As they zeroed in on their prey. My heart, worn down with
Horrors, like coral polyps crumbling under the assault of
Crown of Thorn starfishes, exulted when the canine
(blind to the goodness of its mission) closed on the
Cowering Hamas terrorist (not a militant not a fighter)
And worried at his flailing limbs, just before the posted vid
Reached the end of its running time. This was something
Pure-on an atavistic level-real demons hunted down and
Decimated in their hellish cells like truffles and tubers
Uprooted from the earth by a herd of swine-grubs and
Earthworms down the mole's gullet. The earth that coughed
Up devils with murder and rapine in their hearts, the burrows
Of the *condottiere* of Dis would no more be a haven as the
Israeli army cleaned them out, one by one. Light would
Find them-Light would own them/clip them back like
Deadly nightshade, water hemlock or castor bean.

And yet, how much better to have been pulled down
By The Holy Spirit-the hate-filled heart, the blood-muzzed
Mind cleaned by Salvation and Repentance's welding rod:
The Old Man/Old Life of Troglodyte charters and missals
Buried in the grave-loam and shattered concrete, replaced

By the Christ-driven command: Love Your Neighbor As
Yourself. Finer than the glow of a war-dog's Go-Pro
Would have been the evil man coming out of the fog of
Racial hate and atrocity like a bee-eater bird from out of
Its burrow, soul taking wing, *Abba, Abba* on his lips.
How our tears would have flowed if all over Gaza,
As the earth's tremblors had spat up the sleeping saints
At Calvary, if we could have witnessed the exhumation of
New Lives, dispensing with the lineaments of death's
Doctrines, The Good News on their lips, the balaclavas
And uniforms reviled and forsaken.

What a miracle that would be: to see the craven slayers
Emerge from the darkness of their souls like the
New cicadas from the skin of maple and cherry,
Flushed out with the tongues of Pentecostal fire
Bright as road-flares fuming over their heads,
Professing the divinity of Christ, repenting their evil
Against the Children of Abraham, Kalashnikovs and
Rocket-launchers tossed down at their feet, giving
Themselves up to justice-surrendering to the IDF and
To Christ-as gophers up-flung by the hose in the burrow,
Hands raised to The Son and the sun-Philistia's shame
And mind moored to horror's improvisation sideswiped
By Belief's golden alchemy, by Love's redress, darkness
Swapped for light-hate's roach-holes cleared/Lamb Lamp
Leading death's cult to the road to life-I would I could see it.

Because stygian battles between good dogs and
Human devils with good dogs triumphant, are, ultimately,
Stygian battles between good dogs and human devils,
War without light, war without end.

I look forward to a world without war dogs.
I look forward to a world without tunnels.

HOSTAGE POSTERS

Watching you all, the young and old, bibbers of the River Lethe,
Heedless drinkers of underworld wafts of Oblivion, ripping the
Hostage Posters from walls, light poles, your faces smug or opaque
With the determination of self-righteous bigotry, I can't help
But imagine I can see the ashes and soot of the camp chimneys
Between your eager fingers, rubbed into your cheeks and
Forehead. You recite the lies as you tear up paper's imprimatur
Of stolen souls-some still dully shining in bondage like torchlight
Fishes or comb-jellies in sea-dark-while others have lofted,
Long lost from life, in transit-in queue moon-side of the green kingdom
Of hope and motion. How can we look at you stride from one
Building to sign to brimming kiosk to notice board and
Not hear the jollity of jackboot cadence/catch prescience's echoes of
The glass-smash of another *Kristallnacht*-what was once
Inconceivable here-inexpressible-it's all too easy to picture now.
You rail about decolonization, apartheid, genocide, occupation, catching
The poster-culls on your phone as selfies, while someone, disbelieving,
Appalled, outraged, paces alongside you-*filming you* as you film;
As they record your acts of vandalization, they harangue and mutter,
"No heart, no heart. Nothing moves you as you pull another face down:
The desperate plea for someone to remember, pray for-*remember*
(Kidnapped/Kidnapees/Vermisst) someone's baby, son, daughter,
Father, mother-and you move in a visible darkness split by bilious green of
Withcfire/swamp-gas/unthinking hate's cheap-sheen of St. Elmo's Fire.
"Propaganda," you insist defensively as you hug the posters to your chest,
Looking for a trash receptacle to bin them. "Israel is a genocide state."

And we hear, over and over, quiet as a cymbal's shiver:

"No heart. No heart."

AUTUMN TWILIGHT

I have had dreams of walking with my wife hand in hand,
Across a twilit field of glassine wheat shellacked with
Shadow black as whale oil and the rose-mauve of sunset's
Gradual deference to dusk. We navigate the vast burnished
Weald-a few hayricks here and there arranged like a board
Of Stratego board pieces-and the girls are small girls again and
They are happily leading, holding jars filled with the winking
Foundry jewels of fireflies, which they will release before we
Arrive home which is a half-mile or so ahead-someone is inside
Our country manse, because we can make out the glow of orange panes.
Someone is there. Someone beloved is there: preparing dinner or
Sitting on a stool next to the warmth-pouring hearth, tuning a violin.
Maybe there are others nursing mugs and instruments, and my
Wife's ukelele case propped next to a chair. We are close to the
Beginning of the end of harvest-but not quite there when
Bonfires fume and fiddles sizzle and youths and maids steal kisses
Behind the sheaf-carts; the oldsters raising their hands and
Giving thanks to god for a good harvest beneath the fox-pelt shine
Of the great harvest moon. We are not there: which is alright.

And we all savor the slow walk home and the ease with which
Dusk takes the fields row by row, and rose and mauve give way to the
Washed-out aetheric pinks and blue pastels of the evening's advent.
Fireflies the green of baleful tiger eyes twist upwards in
Dazzling helicals while crow-cuss, grackle-quark and owl-hoot
Rides the cold thread of a light October wind. The stalks talk their
Whispery argot and gad back and forth like Geiger-counter

Arrows. Crickets chirp and tremolo all around us in the
Wind-bent sea; a killdeer goes by, banking, crying its singular cry
Which seems to be for the benefit of the big yellow hunter's moon.
There is the taste of Indian fry-bread and cherry cobbler
On the tongue- and the delicious October tang of homemade
Apple cider-a gift from the neighbors with whom we have been visiting.
And we know there are friends waiting for us back at the house.
I do not know who the neighbors are or who the friends are, or
How we won this interstice of country-time: it is a dream of the
Peace of the year's end, and its magic cannot be dissected or explained.
The country-house, this field, this time is merely a tableau won from
The mind's *Locus coeruleus* imbued with the twilit beauty of one of
Jeremy Lipking's wonderful Southwest paintings.

And I am walking with my wife and her hand is in mine.
And the killdeer cries and a crow or two uncrumple their
Black construction paper lives and wing off north towards
Thick woods and the children wave their magic-jars, their heads barely clearing
The wheat's whickered dance-up-gusting more firefly candescence
From the crop which has only been grazed by the reaper's kiss,
Bug-light's green burr bright as the bioluminescence of some
Sundry of sea-krill, plankton or anglerfish's Coleman glow.
If I turn my head to look at my wife, she will smile at me and I
Will reach out and push aside the wind-disordered dark tresses
From her lips and cheek and feel the impress of her lashes and I will
Think to myself this is a fair twilight and a good dream and
There is the magic of marriage-kiss and children's laughter,
Firefly light brighter than jade fillets and there is the rise of the
Hunter moon's vast yellow disk and delicious impinge of starshine.
There's enough light in twilight's magic-hour and in wheat's
Wand-patter and shadow's deep and tantalizing drift

To imagine

Being surprised in the rows by a brindled tabby with a miniature lamplighter
Hanging from his collar-a glowing amethyst outspreading its beautiful bruised
Purple light-the cat's eyes wonderful emerald enigma reckoning ours for a sec
Before it plods on past us, tail upraised and flicking away galaxies of midges,

Fireflies and baby hoppers, and hanging from its jaws, a great vole or mouse
In russet short-pants, slouch hat on its small head and miniature mandolin and
Scroll case slung across its rodent's back.

To imagine

The stalks parting somewhere off to the right revealing a rag of scarlet fox mask
Hiding the face of a small boy hunkered down amidst the rows-gone with the
Next stingy binge of breeze.

To imagine

In the distance near the wood's verge, where the rows end against the big oaks,
A stout old man in work clothes, hair and beard white as the long day's laze
Of cumulus scud, a semaphore of sickle's blade tied to his waist,
Watching us, marking us as we progress through the glassine sea
As if to say

This is a fair twilight and a good dream, pass on, pass on,
For there is warmth in your home, supper laid out, friends
Laying out their instruments for a good after-sup set
And wine and cider to raise and quaff before they head home.
Listen to killdeer, listen to owl, listen to the wheat's chuff and sigh
Because its dreaming of the reaper's blade and hunter's moon

Your wife's hand is in your own and there are fireflies to guide
You to your porch

Pass on, pass on

This is a fair twilight and a good dream

GOAT-DANCES AND WHITE ROSES

I am so sick so sick of the day's surfeit of horrors and hate,
Like a black goat standing on its back hooves,
Capering towards us, blazing pentagram burned into
Its forehead, eyes burning like coal, hair shiny as grackle,
Lips skimmed back from its big square teeth,
Poised to speak Chaldean-poised to descant in Assyrian,
Determined to crush our desire to make our rendezvous
With *Elohim* and Light. It is not hard to imagine
Some black goat of atrocities auguries declaiming
Through its yellow crust of castanet grin:

We're all boots on the ground, none of us are going to
Say but let us go into the swine, we're all boots on the ground
And there is nothing you can do about it. It is our time, it is
Our season, turn, turn, turn. We (legion) all have homes,
Thrice-dusted, thrice-aired-we (legion) are all boots on
The ground. What will you do? Look at the Hamas fighter
Filming himself holding the Israeli baby with one arm,
The Kalashnikov in the other, grinning through his
Balaclava. Look at the students on their campuses
Screaming "genocide the Jews!"

We are dancing, we are goat-dancing in the noon day sun,
There are black sabbats everywhere-everyone swilling spider wine.
We are boots on the ground and it is our season, turn, turn, turn.
Black sun, black harvest-our time, turn, turn, turn.
When the going gets dark, the dark of heart get going.

What will you do?

I answer back:

I am going to trust in my God, who is a fortified tower
In the face of the enemy and I am going to pray for the
Peace of Jerusalem.

And I just bought a dozen white roses to surprise my wife
When she returns home from work.
What do you think of them?

JOHNNY QUEST/COMPTOM 1969

Raised on Johnny Quest, we boys formed bike packs
And after school, we flew down our South Central streets,
And scoured every abandoned lot that we could find,
Looking for brackish, bubbling pools of potentially lethal
Quicksand, or mini tar-pits. We scooped the earth from the backyard
Or fields gone to thistle and goldenrod, hell-bent on some trace of
Dinosaur fossil that the archaeologists had somehow overlooked,
Buried treasure-human skulls, triple-chained vampire caskets,
A bullet-punched briefcase with a rusty handcuff hanging from the handle.
We buried squads and platoons of green plastic American grunts
In the earth and after a while, forgot where we put them, as if
They were obligatory sacrifices to The God of Petroleum
Who demanded return of his loan of plastics from time to time.
And we searched, beneath the house foundation crawlspaces
For Gila Monsters, with the zeal of good old King Pellinor
Pursuing the Questing Beast, and for baby pterodactyl carcasses
Squirreled away in the husks of dead trees, imagining we'd
Stumble across their wing-wrapped forms-dry and dark as
Old jerky or carob pods-light as box-kites.

Sadly, though none of these wonders existed.

But shrunken heads (ah, man childhood nightmare!)
Shrunken heads
Could be had for a few cents
From the Newberry's and Sears department stores
Down the road.

RUSSIAN PRESIDENT VLADIMIR PUTIN/ AUTUMN DREAMS 2023

How often do you quaff the Lethe's chill vintage of Oblivion,
To forget dead eyes-rolled up, like poached bass or sturgeon,
Sclera gone the slightly blue-tinged hue of a swimmer's lips,
In plentitude like pearls in a beauty's woven basket on Fair Day,
Shining up at you, bright as mercury, in your dreams?
Do you leaven nightmares of screen rataplan of staff reports,
Ground gained, ground lost-some God-rumble of rubble
Promising future judgment with visions of pinions of
Byzantine eagles and wolfs' heads on saddlebows of Ivan's Oprichniks?
Does the Old Dragon who has fed your dragon dreams,
Send the long-dead drake, Zmey Gorynych, he who earned
A new head (he had three) for every hundred years of life,
To speak with serpent's sibilance: think of the faces of
Your women-stashed all over the Federation like illicit
Bank accounts-and take heart that the Americans are
Cutting Zelensky's funding off. Did you, *Veliki Knez* of terrors
See the scaly horror nodding his three heads in the midst of
His gout/glam of fire couch like some clockwork Ghidorah,
And mumble to yourself: *yes, the Americans can't keep it going,*
I just have to stay the course-the money has to stop, it has to.
The man's begging for cash now like a faith-healer on one of those
Old-time American telethons. Yes, Zmey is right, Zmey is right.

Did you smile and drift off into seamless dreams,
Without fulgence of icon eye/blackness of fuming armor,

The whine of conscience no more than autumn's riffle
In the russet crowns of Moscow's spruces, oaks and hornbeams,
Qualms fading like the quick wink of a beluga's blue eye
Beneath a pleat of Black Sea surf?

BLACK TURBAN SNAIL SHELL

Like snow dusting the top

Of a volcano's crater

These whorls of nacre

On the rise of the black turban's shell.

JAPANESE FIRE MAPLE

This morning, I returned from work, and it was darned cold:
The sun hadn't cast its lure for the gold honey gouramis,
Yellow platys, marigold swordtails and other small fries of light
Swimming in the green frost-tinged lawn. And as I walked stiffly
Up the cement walkway to my front door, I looked over at the front
Planter at the Japanese fire maple-the deciduous tree we planted
A year or so back, and it saddened me to see it stripped of its
Red-purple leaves-its fireglow (Acer Palmatum) truly tamped;
The bad-bruise embers well and gone as merciless winter worked
Its will. The few fingery leaves that remained were folded in on
Themselves, shriveled as bats hanging from a barn's beams.
And I felt a little bit colder, seeing our young tree bereft
Of its blaze, but as I regarded its faded crimson-purple
Tinctures an image came to me from when I was young

And I smiled
As I remembered:

The Replacements concert my brother and some friends
Attended in Los Angeles back in the 90s and, next to me,
Rocking out with the rest, was a young woman with
A voluminous tumble of red-raspberry hair, eyes sparkling as
She looked up into those of her boyfriend, her smile blindingly
Bright as sunfire on morning snow as she mouthed the lyrics to t
The song the band was playing:

"Next Saturday morning in church I'll give you away
In my eyes happy tears I can't hide on your wedding day."

And I smiled-the stripped tree, the winter chill and bone aches
Forgotten-as I headed for the front door to greet *my wife* and my children.

The Japanese fire maple will grow and flourish, gaining in beauty
And abundance.

I hope the same is true of the love between the woman with
The wine-colored locks and her man.

THOSE DAYS

Thank God for childhood-for the days when the sky
Was bluer than cornflowers and the grass in the backyard
Where plastic army men and dinosaurs fought their ancient grudge
Was transformed by the eye of imagination into primal arboreal
Giants choked with lianas, and holes and depressions became
Steaming mangrove swamps of low drifting mist and fog
From which a giant rubber spider or alien might spring and
Take down a dogface armed with a bazooka, carbine or M-16.
Remember: Tyrannosaurus Rex always fought on the side
Of the Axis, with an assist from Pteranodon, while
Stegosaurus, Triceratops and Ankylosaurus favored the Allies,
While the plastic-rubber aliens filled in as neutrals and reserves.
Thank Him for the Tamiya scale WWII models you worked on
Outside on the picnic table next to the big elm, and the gray
And black tabby that you sort of owned but didn't picking
Its way through the long grass to check out what you were
Up to-startling when an orange dragonfly or sparrow would
Zip overhead and you could hear the distant tinkle of the
Ice cream truck's chimes drifted over from the next street.

Give gratitude to the God who put it in your heart to
Run in exhausting circles then throw yourself down on the lawn,
Dizzy and disoriented, looking at the heavens' vast gullet,
Sure that gravity would reverse itself as you lay there, winded,
Clutching the green blades in your hands: that you would
Sail up like a balloon into the afternoon's vast porcelain blue.
Thank Him for the friends that showed up after dinner and

Asked if you could come out and play-and off you would go,
Part of a bike pack zipping through the endless network of
Neighborhood streets-leaders and game-plans changing on
The whims of the majority, the teasing comments made to the
Girls hanging out in front of their homes-their rejoinders lost
As, amidst gaggles of laughter, you put on speed to
Round the nest corner. Thank the God who knew you before He
Knit you in your mother's womb for the baseball games
You played in the middle of the road, and the patient motorists
Who waited for you to move aside-and then back you went;
For the providential jingles of ice-cream trucks that brought
Children running from practically every house on the street,
Change jingling in their fists.

Thank God for the tangelo sunsets and buttermilk clouds
Of yellow at the day's end, the worn glove on your hand,
The ball in the other, while you told yourself over and over,
Watching the day's burnish set the big buildings and
Telephone poles blazing, the block's life ticking down
In car backfires, dog talk and kids yelling to each other as they
Blasted by on their bikes reflectors showing their red-amber
Flints

Tomorrow, tomorrow will be even better. There will always
Be days like this. Let there always be days like this.

XI JINPING GENERAL SECRETARY OF THE CHINESE COMMUNIST PARTY/AUTUMN DREAMS 2023

Honestly, I do not want to delve into your dreams-the soul's miasma
Pressed into your pillow-I see them in my waking hours, the dregs of
The dolorous bird-droppings from your *locus coeruleus*, from whatever
Blue Spot (as the Romans would call it) from which you dream horrors
And aggressions towards my nation. Unlike our President, you would
Never be a stop-boot in the Gate of Ivory-where our Old King Ahab,
Joseph Biden remains enslaved by the deceiving visions of the
Treacherous shades of the chthonic Manes. That isn't for you.
Do you imagine golden Chinese dragons barber-poling down
The Red, White and Blue, techno-demons of wing-char and computer chip,
Transistor, iron, chrome, steel, Lithium pit's grave-earth stomping through
Washington's environs? In your dreams, your autumn dreams, do you
See yourself as The Son of Heaven riding Yinglong's golden back,
Flare of scarlet mane in your face, cresting the blue egg of earth,
Stars before you, saluting President Vladimir Putin as he puts the spurs
To his own triple-headed glory-worm, Zmey Gorynych, the latter's
Three heads kowtowing to you? In your dreams, do you say, in a voice
Cold and forbidding as the stellar gulfs: *America is finished and there is*
OEnough for us both, The West is done and there is enough for us both;
Their leaders are bought and sold and their children are a generation of
Castratos and eunuchs-there is enough for us both. And did Yinlong
Exhale the gray effluvium-cirrus of pox and bacillus and Zmey the green
Fog of irradiation-of missile and dirty-bomb as you looked down at the
Blue unwitting globe beneath the fanning pinions of your reptilian steeds?

Did you empty a slop-bucket of dissident's, Christian's and Uighur's blood
Into the jaws of your imperious steed and wink at Putin and his Zmey?
Do you imagine dropping like a curse until you land on Taiwan,
Washington-even Israel?

I wonder if your sleeper's brow is knit with unconscious misgivings and
Doubts-though it all seems to be going your way.

Your nation's youth are not producing children-many have vowed not to do so.

Could it be they have no wish to dream the dream you wish to foist on them and us?

Could it be that there are limits to the awful ambitions of dragons?

Are there limits to nightmares suffered?

KIM JONG UN SUPREME LEADER OF NORTH KOREA/AUTUMN DREAMS 2023/ WINTER DREAMS 2024

It is distressing to see that you are greeting 2024 with dreams of fire;
But can we be surprised, since your dreams in 2023 were much the same?
Like a pudgy Nero praying to presume perfect notes of lyre-fire to fan a holocaust,
Ghastly gifts of Promethean torch-terror to pass Man into nuclear dark,
Here you are, smiling into your pillow, the songs of the azure-winged magpie
And Eurasian skylark still hours away, and in the dream you are on an
Ocean's glaze of parboiled waves-black as tar pleated with lava crust-your bed
Bobbing among the steamed fish and birds, still smoking gray, locked
Together in death like Celtic knotwork as you watch the American coast and
Interior go up in fulminations of molten mushrooms-Autumn skullcaps,
Destroying angels and death caps-as Apollyon's yield descends like hornets
On those whom you do not even know.

Did your father, the last dictator, assure you, before he died, you would do this;
Tell you this was your destiny-to leave The South and America in
Briquet-time, glowing coals of jaguar sclera scattered to the four winds?
("a hemiplegic malformation and colonial subordinate state" whose society is
("tainted by Yankee culture": your words about the South quoted today).
Things are going badly for the Yankees, it's true with porous borders,
Gender Ideology run amok, national division, antisemitism in the halls
Of education, economic sorrows and military contretemps-well, the
Dreams of Joe Biden-do you ever dream of *him* trapped in the Door of Horn,
Filling up like a mylar balloon with the deceiving words of the chthonic Manes?
In the depths of slumber when you dream of the nuclear hell you wish to
Rain down on your enemies, do you see yourself astride the back of a
Great dragon, the 81 scales of the yang substance glowing beneath your saddle,
The fabled orb of omnipotence and creation, the *Cintimani* grasped in its fangs?

Do you dream of dragons and dragonfire as Putin dreams of Zmey Gorynych,
And Jingping dreams of Yinlong-of joining your dragon's fire with their own
Against your enemies, the earth below your steed's pinions transformed into
Black clouds belching scarlet? Do they whisper to you in the argot of dragons
And dragon-riders:

Now, now, this is the hour-hoped for, sought for, longed for we will never
Have a better chance yes the hour hoped for, sought for, longed for

Will you greet The New Year with New Fire, you and your friends?

When you wake from these visions, do you stroke a length of hip from a
Compelled bedmate peeking from the disordered covers, circle a dimple on
A moon-striped buttock, run your fingers through tresses of silken grackle black?
Peeking from

Or is love and sex for that matter the poor man's Taekwondo, when its set
Against the anticipation of radiation's chartreuse kisses?

SAN FRANCISCO CLEANS UP FOR XI

Xi arrived, and Gavin, gov, he, earning fee,
Took lye and soap to San Fran's dying polity,
And from the streets, the wretched, mad and needled knaves,
That camped and cloured, died and dropped in teeming waves,
He whisked away, lest he who shed the Uighur's blood,
Should place his shoe upon their fecal'd fanes and crud,
And find offense, when crossing on the sidewalk's breadth,
Should look askance upon the mother felled by meth,
Or fentanyl-the child skinned by famine's wrack,
For Xi was here-in auspicies we cannot lack!
And up they went his scarlet flags and stars of gold,
Those vaunted rags-the ensigns of oppression's wold,
Upon those streets where stours stilled to mark their fame,
While sense and safety guttered like a votive flame,
They snapped and eeled, they lofted 'bove the common weal,
Who cheered and jeered to see their silken swifts anneal.

Then why the stint on fuller's soap and bleaching spray,
Before, when parents, dreading the morn of school's assay,
Would walk their sons and daughters past the soiled yurts,
And boxes where the schizophrenic bawled his hurts;
Who clears the pissers from the dining table's reach,
Proffers the physic for disorder-oh, some leech!
And what the merchant, sweeping 'side the broken glass,
Who mourns his losses, watching cops give scums their pass,
And shutters up the goods and produce of his work,
And counts the coins and dollars to his trembled clerk?

Were they, the citizens unworthy of disport,
Of cleaning agents cast upon the vile cohort,
But needs must bear the squalor with placidity,
With no relent, except for high diplomacy?
Oh-how it smarts and how it fills the gorge with galls,
To mime Potemkin's shacks among the broken stalls.

How sad the city, like a hag in fever cloth,
Its breath a whisp-the tambour of a deathshead moth,
Should rouse itself and to the marred show unmarred streets,
When smoking tar and oil best attend such greets,
And sweet bouquets offered up in friendly moil,
Replaced by hemlock and nightshade's noxious coil.
And those that force decrees and fiats with the maul,
And force their folk to wear the collar of the thrall,
How little they commend the hyssop and the sage,
While those who cope with stink and fetor pay the wage,
Bearing the madman's rant and addict's contumely,
Receiving little aid and sparse security,
Must spit and grumble seeing this is small abate,
In pox and felons coming with the morrow's freight.
Who loves the ones who living here, support the loam
And laws of the beleaguered vale they call their home,
And ask of leaders probity in governance,
Not smuts and excrements in doleful recompense,
But half a span to raise their kids and work in peace,
Their streets and blocks disfavored of its ambergrease.

Xi arrived, and Gavin, gov, he, earning fee,
Took lye and soap to San Fran's dying polity.
And from the streets, the wretched, mad and needled knaves,
That camped and cloured, died and dropped in teeming waves,
He whisked away, lest he who shed the Uighur's blood,
Should place his shoe upon their fecal'd fanes and crud.

     TODD FRENCH

AUTUMN DREAM

Autumn dream/moon-striped horses/breathing in/breathing out fireflies.

WINTER

MORNING/12/11/23

God is cancelling the pre-dawn dark: He has yanked out
His sketchpad and is inking in the moon's muddy cat/rabbit prints,
Etching the brown thrust of a fig branch and blue bordured
Green of the fingery leaves. Look at that! He just jotted off a black phoebe
Sitting at the poolside, quick as a gunslinger slapping leather!
Now he's filling in a hunk of gold vellum scroll roll on the air,
Dotted with bird note; there's a pointillist bit of scarlet for
The one red pepper in the planter, and the sky's molybdenum
Is being replaced with peach-rose and whisps of indigo cloud.
Ah, what would you give to see the old tuxedo cat dashed off
In mid-stalk on the backyard brick-first some floating whiskers,
Then the head, an uplifted paw, the haunches, body and
The periscope tail set against the cross-hatched branches of
The Japanese privet-the leaves touched with morning's mellow
Mead-drizzle.

When night falls, He will wad the art up in His stellate hands
And bank it into a hoop of coal-sack black.

Come next morning, He'll begin anew.

EUROPA

I am thinking of this Idea of America.

It seems to be on its way out.

When it's gone, like Europa borne away on the bull-back and clods of Zeus, it's gone;
No redo: we will not be drag-footing after *that idea* like Cadmus, giving up the quest and
Compensated with a second Thebes-dreaming of this America as he must have dreamt of
His sister hot-hoofed away by her toxic-bovine-Olympian rapist; he must have imagined
Her in the rags of her Phoenician silks of purple and blue, hair streaming behind her,
Her eyes rolling with terror, sweat flying from her neck, her gold-wired locks flying
Behind her like wind-driven rags of sable cloud-a vision turned over to the remorseless
Piston and buck of lathered beast/god muscle. She must have always hung tantalizingly
Before his vision even in the drifts of sleep-after he was requited with a crown, with
Cities and warriors up-jumped like corn shoots from the alien earth; the blood and gore of
Monsters smoking on his sword. Was it really sufficient compensation for the failure of the
Sister-quest: were his dreams, as he tossed between the perfumed flanks of beautiful
Illyrian consorts, ever free of the mirage of the maiden, head turned, beseeching,
Hands fastened to the cruel horns like a bosun's on the mast amidst a storm-pleated
Sea? Was the image of the purloined sibling always before his eyes straddling the bull that
Was white as a beluga splitting/riding/sliding/chuffing through the waves on its way to
Crete-or was the hero, the city-founder, dragon-slayer relieved to have never caught
Up with the sky god *because we all know how that tussle would have ended.*
Be that as it may, his conscience must have been pricked by the mission's failure,
His inner gaze held by the saunter of flower-wound horns knifing through the high surf,

Charging through the billows-hide black and vast as a herd of pinnipeds.
The city-founder must have tossed and turned, the Gone Girl's voice distant as
Gull-gab amidst the breakers-blotted out by the bassoon brogue of wave and wind;
The dead duty of retrieval must have shamed him now and then-like the rake of a
Piscine eye of a dried bonito caught in a net. He knew he hadn't wanted to come to grips
With The Thunderer-thunders dressed in cowskin-but he must have felt the sister-theft
Keenly even with the flood of glories and achievements spread before him.
The pain of loss was plain as the tide-tossed petals from the garlands she had
Placed on the cruel bone sheaths of keratin. Did the conflict of kidnap without
Closure work at him like Zeus' hoof pawing away at the sand? Everywhere he
Turned, did he summon up the lowered horns?

How could he forget her?

How could he afford to rescue her?

In my own way, as I watch things play out in this nation, I am getting use to the
Notion that the country I knew is, like Europa, fading from view: its freedoms and
Liberties, its mission and responsibilities of moral arbitration on the world-stage,
Now wafted away-gotten away by the God that gave it everything and rejected by a
Gen Z which believes it isn't worth fighting for. What is happening is a hurtful
And prolonged Farewell without redress, without hope.

Like a hero standing on Phoenicia's shore, mourning the loss of a sibling, I am
Sadly contemplating the ruler-straight meet of sea and sky, mind's eye fixed on
The fading white of dead wakes-the sea-muffled cries of someone who deserved
To be saved.

WINTER WEEDING

Though a cold breeze was coming in from the mountains,
The rains were done and I decided to make the most of it by doing some
Weeding in the backyard planter that runs along the dividing wall
To the left. As I bent down to pull some milkweed from the
Earth, a big yellow Cloudless Sulfur butterfly flounced over the
Pink bricks: the hue of an indigent's raddled nicotine dream or some
Sour memory of Bad Love given an assist by a pitying angel's pinion.
I froze, the greens in my mud-streaked hands forgotten, and watched
The insect zig-zag in the air until it disappeared over the back wall.
I straightened up, standing on the ground bereft of autumn's gourds,
And reflected that there is room enough in this world now and then
For a bit of bruised grace.

ANTSY CHILDREN/CHRISTMAS MORNING
12/25/23

Please Lord, even with conflicts spanning the globe,
Soldiers humming Mars' sour refrain for their carols,
And Peace, like the albatross, seldom touching down
On this terrene world: please God, let there be antsy children,
Excited-up early-eyes shining with wonder, joy and anticipation

On Christmas Morn.

WINTER CLOUDS

I am heading back home on the 405 S and I am glorying
In the last vestiges of morning rain clouds-isolated friezes of great
Clots, curds and whipped meringues of purple, indigo blue,
White, gray-reminding me of the cumulus cram in a
Max Parrish or N.C. Wyeth painting or the implosions of
Such in the wonderful anime of Makoto Shinkai. They are being
Swept out to sea or east to the Saddleback Mountain.
These are blowsy mothers who were delivered of their babes last night
And in the early morn-hard labors-they all had hard labors!
Their birth pains were expressed in tearing basso organ chords,
Ripping sonic rataplans of brash Cathedral-speak-sky bumble of
Thunder-like the death-throes of pine, blue fir and larch when the
Two-man crosscut saw has its way. And the tears-how they poured!
They hammered the roof of our home in a never-ending assault of
Bullet hard drops-and that of my work-post during my shift;
Ah, there was no mercy for these ladies abed in birth's stour,
All of them belly-cut with cruel Caesarians-God denied them
Easy births even this close to that of His precious Son; but the storms
Passed and not one of them could say they grieved a stillborn.
The thirsty earth-flower, tree, plant and shrub-was grateful,
Meadow, dale, vale, forest, city, block and hamlet thanked them
For their sorrows, for their wearying dilations, contractions and breaches.
Now they are chockful with milk, brimming with joy-scudding down
Heaven's robin blue halls with their infants at their chests,
Their husbands waiting to take them home.

They are heading seaward to recover.

Like wild Highland dames, they are heading for mountain and hill to recover.
We are done, they say. We are done: we are just done.

MORNING RAINS/12/31/23/MARSHLANDS

It is the Lord's Day and my heart is with the Word,
But it's also with the marshlands over at HB Central Park.
As the rain falls lightly, I am wondering if the black-necked
Stilts are stalking through the mud and water-grass, plunging
Their black bill-spikes into the precipitation-churned morass,
Their rose-pink legs shellacked with mud and mire. I wonder if the
Deer-colored curlews and whimbrels from the coast are
In the mix, making their way through the cold mulch with the
Patient, robotic steps of a bomb-squad looking for IEDs.
Of course we can expect quarrelsome Egyptian geese, colorful wigeons,
Mallards and their dams put-putting across the swollen,
Pleated waters, and the haughty white and blue herons,
Off-standish as divas or teenage ballerinas secure in
The knowledge of their infinite grace. I am thinking of
Putting on my walking shoes a bit later, and if the weather
Permits, maybe heading out to enjoy the beauty of the
Rain-drenched green and black shiny boughs of pine,
Sycamore, oak and cherry-and the soothing tick-tick-tick
Od raindrops from limb and branch joined by the tentative strains
Of California towhee, yellow warblers and hooded orioles.
Joggers and dog-walkers will be doing their thing and
The Butterfly Garden, even shorn of its sunflowers at
This time of year, will boast its blooms even in the face of
Winter's icy blasts, and the park alive with hydrangeas blue
As a baby's bonnet-fiery trumpet vines, lantana the colors of
Madagascar gems. And all their colors amplified by the
Meeting of water's bright beads with leaf/petal/feather; there are

Few balms like the quietude of nature after a rain-shower,
Watching the sky low-altitude clots of dusty cumulus speed by.

Maybe I will catch a glimpse of a quick ferruginous missile of
Hawk as it beats wing above the tops of the great eucalyptus trees.
But really, the marsh area is on my mind and the
Delicious peace to be found in the scrape and whisper
Of reeds/cattails under the pall of a sky of frosted-grass gray,
Or when frigates of clouds the ash-black of ibis and boat-tailed grackle
Pass overhead, bringing decent gusts and more sprinkles.
If Frog=Perfection, but I have never heard the frogs sing
In the shallows and green overgrown banks because I
Never come here when the full moon barrels through the
Rags of fleeing clouds, the candescence of its gold corona
Outshining the stars. I am not like as to visit the park at
Night in the chance to appreciate the free concerts of green,
Bull and southern leopard frog.
Even so, I wonder, what kind of seabirds might I see today.

MORNING RAINS/12/31/23

Raindrops fall
Leaves allow
Snare-drum's shiver
God's good music

BLUE POISON DART FROG

Wow: just take a look at the gloss
On that blue poison dart frog and tell me
If that isn't some gorgeous
Medicine for Melancholy-one last Sake sip
From an Edo Kiriko cobalt cup

MORNING OF NEW YEAR'S DAY/01/01/24

The New Year

Not off

To a good start:

Earth tremors.

BELISARIUS

He fought valiantly for the ungrateful Roman Emperor Justinian,
Often under the umbra of base jealousy, on a shoestring, bearing
Aspic-tongued Theodora's undeserved criticism, and the
Cuckold's horns courtesy of his wife Antonia. He bore the hurts
Like the giant Atlas the world-whether routing the German Vandals
And their Moorish levies in North Africa-or winning much of Italy
From the Goths. He often did it with a dollop of troops and courage:
Ballless Narses, the eunuch would finish the affair, blessed with the
Troops and gold that should have gone to the great general.
Belisarius served selflessly, never made a grab for the Purple,
Took the abuse from the home-front at Constantinople like the
Martyr Stephen stood and took the stoning when the Pharisees and coat-holding
Saul did him in. The Goths tried to tempt him with the sweetmeats
Of crown and homage and he used the ruse of acceptance before
Marching into Ravenna in triumph. But he stayed true, even when the Empress,
An ex-prostitute with a circus bear-training dad, laid into him without
Cause, and Justinian gave what should have gone to him to his
Enemies, even denying him a second Triumph. When kings
See laurels on the heads of others they see red like bulls getting
Their first eyeful of the matador's scarlet *muleta*. There are No
Grateful Princes-just whisper-galleries and gratitude grudging as
A lean rib tossed to a starving dog-or a passing flare of sunset's
Rose on a chink of mosaic tile. They hectored, impoverished and
Benched him off and on-and he took it in stride-or as best he could,
Always on the cusp of heartbreak, but never demoralized to the
Point of pursuing treason and revolution. I wonder if the general
Ever sat in the rain and ash-shellacked entry of his tent in his

Camp chair and had a secretary read the beseeching psalms of
David to him as he brooded on his hurts. Maybe, as he shifted and
Rubbed at an armor-abraded shoulder or checked a furrow of healing
Gash on his leg, he had someone read to him from Homer's *Iliad*,
Of the quarrels between Agammemnon and the far-runner,
Valiant Achilles as they fell out with one another-egged on by
Capricious divinity-over the Trojan War.

What he must have thought when he was trying to regain
Fire-gutted Rome and the lost western half of the empire for
His ungrateful liege:

When had the ex-courtesan who had ducks nibble birdseed off

Her body ever laced up a cuirass, ridden hard miles against a foe,
Fought in the thick of the press, or stood a siege-to train herself
To stare owl-eyed at horrors and keep wading into the fray,
Sword in hand?

For that matter, when had Justinian done the same?

What did they know about facing death, going without food or sleep,
Hunting men with steel through cities turned into firebreaks and
Wolf's haunts?

It never stops–they just keep the abuse coming like the marsh coot hooting,
Like the bull-frogs at night–it just never stops never stops never stops

Sometimes I wonder if God inflicted it all on this honest soldier
Because, earlier, he and his subordinates had gone full horror-show on
The folks in the Hippodrome arena when the charioteer factions,
The Blues and Greens, had mutinied against Justinian. Belisarius
And the troops had hacked away without discrimination, as the
Emperor Theodosius' troops had against the Thessalonicans in the circus.
How many innocent victims, caught in the bloody mulch, fathers,
Mothers, sons and daughters, had gone down before the blades,
Begging for mercy, all because the Blues and Greens had joined
Together in insurrection and even crowned a pretender? Blood
Doesn't sleep and the God that hears it crying from the ground is a
Holy and Righteous God and *you know that blood never sleeps.*

Was that why the sword of unearned fault-finding, blood-clots
Of men and money had fallen on Belisarius' house?

The chronicles do not agree on his last days. Some say he ended
Down-at-his-heels, blinded by Justinian, led by a boy, begging
Coppers from the men he once led. Other sources affirm that he
Ended his days in a decent palace given to him by a remorseful
Emperor after Theodora had passed on. Compassion moves me to hope
That it was the latter–with the palace shrew planted in her sepulcher–the
Two of them made up and talked about the Old Days, when they were
In accord and the working relationship hadn't become as poisonous
As a cup of aged hemlock, the words as brutal as toxic as a hail of
Curare darts.

If there is a patron saint for our veterans sleeping on benches,
In cardboard boxes in garbage-hemmed lots–the-stink of spoiled
Oranges and fish in their lungs each morn–I don't know a better one
Than the old general who had borne the vagaries of fortune like
Boil-pocked Job sitting in the dust scraping himself with postsherds.
Belisarius would have understood their curses and prayers,
Their PTSD, their traumas and wounds–he would have felt for
Each and every one of them–the wounded warriors who saw action

TODD FRENCH

In Afghanistan, Kuwait, Iraq, Vietnam-he would have known what
It was like to be forsaken, to be unappreciated, mocked and disdained,
Cast into penury and ignominy. To be the victim of an incompetent
And unfeeling civil bureaucracy-to be wished into insignificance
Like a dust-devil in the dooryard, like the refuse bags on the
Street corners.

He would have understood the sack-covered bottles and discarded
Needles. The shakes and the sweats.

The general-whether he went to heaven or hell with two eyes or
No eyes, would have know what it was like to be *forsaken*.
Cast out without a canteen like Hagar in the wilderness.

He would have understood the sobs of those watching the abandonment
Of Afghanistan to the despicable Taliban and the tear-strangled words
Of disbelief and anger:

Oh my God, how could they?
My God, my God, how could they?

PAUL

When he stood vigilance over the coats of the stone-throwers,
Zealous as any Quebecois over a pile of pelts waiting
For a good price, how could he foresee the day when the
Rocks would rain down on him-when eyes un-gummed and
Alight with the knowledge of Christ, emerging from the
Rubble of his old life, in the context of great pain, he would
Look at the world-at Truth-with eyes clear and wide as a tarsier's
Knocked out of its tree?

THE MARTYR STEPHEN

How could someone anyone be so God-filled with love,
Even for the stone-throwers, the murderous, hypocritical Pharisees,
Taking his life from him without cause at the city's limits,
To breath those words through blood, life-candle's gutter,
The thud of rock against flesh, against bone. How could anyone
Faced with faces rift in hate's rictus, arms rising and falling
Like anemone tendrils or Antarctic Sun Starfish to deal the
Next blow-how could anyone find it at the moment of death,
To say: "Lord, do not hold this sin against them." I am shaken
And humbled by the Martyr Stephen's forgiveness of his killers
As I am by Christ's "Forgive them, Father," or the quiet in the
Storm's eye moment during the crucifixion when the Centurion
Before the Cross says, "Surely, this was the Son of God."
Reading this in the context of The Age of Unforgiveness when
Past Sin gets you cancelled by the godless-there can never be
Forgiveness in the Left's eyes, just a redder and better
Jacquerie cap-or someone's reach for the empyrean expressed
Through a Mother/Child roadside bomb-a knife brandished against
A writer who speaks the intolerable to the intolerant. I pondered
This Age of Unforgiveness, in which every opponent's adolescent
Slip-up is pried out of the stone of Man's hard heart like the cicadas
Emerging from the trees or sea-flowers teased from hydrothermal vents,
Like the hand-warmed release of an auklet's chick from its volcano nest,
To be treasured, to be used/used/used when the opportunity is ripe.
When they (the Pharisees) bum-rushed the Man of God to the city limits,
Like antisemite Ivy leaguers descending on a son or daughter of Abraham,
How could they fathom the love-swelled pump of the heart in the

Evangelist that denied the squid's ink of animus and rage that gusted
From their own-and forgave, forgave in the face of their unjust sentence,
Of the ruddy glow of holy murder's storm-light in their eyes?

"Lord, do not hold this sin against them."

In the rock-dented skull, the thought-expansive/unbelievable-caromed;
In the stone-trammeled breast, the God-breathed/God-loving wish
Winged upwards and out like one of Alex Alemany's candescent doves.
Even as he sank beneath hate's unforgiving rain and the body's cell
Release of pain mediators-the prostaglandin, bradykinin, serotonin
Blew out like a gas-fire on a back burner-there was no blood bubble
Of curse on the numb lips-exhaled into the moist dirt-beads of crimson

EARTH.

But I say to you, Love your enemies and pray for those who persecute you, so that you may be sons of your Father who is in heaven. For he makes his sun rise on the evil and on the good, and sends rain on the just and on the unjust.

There was just:

"Lord, do not hold this sin against them."

For if you love those who love you, what reward do you have? Do not even the tax collectors do the same? And if you greet only your brothers,[a] what more are you doing than others? Do not even the Gentiles do the same?

Oh God, my God, that such forgiveness could live in this world!

That such love could live in this land

EPSTEIN'S LIST

Men and women hunger for Justice: it is part of the Garden
Which clings to us in this fallen world-something that reminds us
We were made for something infinitely finer and that joins us
To our Creator-who is a God of infinite justice and righteousness.
It doesn't matter that the power of Evil-armored like the pangolin,
Allows its children-gifted with wealth and prominence,
To curl up in a scale-ball when the light of scrutiny arrives.
They are releasing (the redacted) List (redacted) because there is
Still Justice-like dirty beams streaming down through the dust
Gummed panes of an abandoned church's clerestory windows;
Worrying its way through quake rubble like a service dog looking
For survivors-or a man or woman at the controls of a plane
Looking for one human speck adrift on a vast, wind-whipped sea.

The mills of God grind slow but sure-we tell ourselves between
The atrocity and the airing-the sharing-of what is unspeakable;
The mills of God grind slow but sure-we tell ourselves,
When Dragon Days inveigh and everything vile is dead and buried,
The mills of God grind slow but sure-we tell ourselves,
Between the suicide's noose and the full shine of The Werewolf Moon.
The mills of God grind slow but sure we tell ourselves-between
The insomnia of filthy dreamers and the *whuff-whuff* of the ceiling fan
Over their beds-their sleep interrupted by their remembered gambols
On Tiberius' Capri and the fear of what the morning will bring.

The mills of God grind slow but sure.

The Bad Don't Sleep Well-they hear the cockerel of morning
Every moment of their lives.

Men and women hunger for Justice: it is a part of the Garden,
The Good Flower and Light's lattice-bars which clings to us in this
Fallen world-something that reminds us we were made for something
Infinitely better-that something dear stayed with us even as we were
Turned out to till the fields of our grieving hearts.

The mills of God grind slow but sure.

We want to believe we can hear the heavenly lyre of the
Archangel Gabriel's palate saying: I had to fight the (demon)

Prince of America to arrive here and see The List released,
And when I return home I will have to contend with both the Prince
Of America and the Prince of China, but with Michael's help
I will succeed.

It will out.
Believe it.
It will out.

CRYSTAL COVE/01/09/24/SANDPIPER

Blustery day at the beach.
Grayish-white and blurry as a bad roll of
Television snow, the young sandpiper
Stabs and nibbles its way along this
Stretch of low-tide sand.

CRYSTAL COVE/01/09/24

Wind whipping the whitecaps

Sunfire's semaphore off the charcoal feathers

Of a lone cormorant

CRYSTAL COVE/01/09/24

Unable to help myself

I follow the trail

One red rose

Tossed up

By the tide

Then another

And another

And another

WE WANT YOU TO DO FOR US

Mark 10:35-37
English Standard Version

The Request of James and John
[35] And James and John, the sons of Zebedee, came up to him and said to him, "Teacher,
we want you to do for us whatever we ask of you." [36] And he said to them, "What do
you want me to do for you?" [37] And they said to him, "Grant us to sit, one at your right
hand and one at your left, in your glory."

I can picture the Son of Man suppressing a wry smile when the
Sons of Thunder came to him with their request-approaching the subject
With the sly vagueness of teen youths trying to finagle the keys to the
Car from Dad for the weekend-or old plains buffalo-hunters, dressed
In skins, creeping up on a herd grazing on Montana's turf. But though
They were as cautious as cats in the drifts on Snow Days, how could they
Believe that the God who knew when every sparrow falls from the branch in
Death, trill frozen in its beak-who could hear the aneurysm ballooning in
A blood vessel, wouldn't know what they were going to say before the
Words were formed? The Master loved them, and He explained that the
Gift of sitting at the right and left hand wasn't His to give and He taught them
The difference between being caught up in the blandishments of ego and self
And being the Selfless Servant. Wisdom and humility are gleaned in such ways:
As pitcher plants gather rainwater, or as the desert acacia-in pints or dollops.
Was it not the same as when the brothers wanted to call down Elijah-fire like
A surgical airstrike on the township that wouldn't take Christ and He rebuked
Them with love and patience?

And we love these Apostles, James and John even more for such moments,
More than for all the healings and scattering of demons like scads of
Dust-bunnies, because we can see the fallibility-the flawed human side and
Say to ourselves *well, yes, I can see myself in them,* illimitable Want and
Need for preeminence-yes, the inner eye can catch the small sour flicker of
Jaundiced yellow in the soul's gold and scarlet radiance:

Yes, they are not so different as me.

They are not so different.

And aren't there times-each day-we say to God I want you to do for me...

THE WAR VETERAN ARRIVING IN HEAVEN

Awareness-past the soothing rush-blush of Godlight-of the
New body's sinecure-the glove of empyrean flesh-spirit
Bereft of scars'congeries, courtesy of Ia Drang Valley,
Fallujah, Bucha, Gaza, Chernobyl-everything wholewholewhole,
PTSD unwoven, unseamed and spurned like shroud cloth,
All addictions done-no memory of bottle/memory/pipe,
Dream's miasma of burnt flesh-bone/blood/smoke
Overheated shells/ordnance/body-bag's plastic char
And rubble vapors-zero-gravity gusted away
Stone gardens/Wall names/obelisk/plaque winking out
Like jade fillet shine of starfall-mind's whine of years of
Bench/cardboard bench/benefits hold-ups no more no more

OhmyGodmyGodmyGod

Whole and peace peace peace

Warmthwarmthwarmtheidersoftruffleangelwingnorackandpack

Whole and peace peace peace

WINTER RAIN AND CONCERTINAS/01/20/24

There was music outside the house: the cymbal-shiver of
Rain's rataplan filling the kitchen courtesy of the
Half-open sliding glass door. Occasionally the tremble
Of alloy-bowl's beat would shade rise from its tender
Disc-driven *crotales* to a raucous maraca beat before
Subsiding to its steady cellophane shpiel. Nature's
Band play wasn't big on brass or smoky sax, but it was
Restful and sedate and we get so little rain these days that
It was an ecstasy to disregard the gelid creep in the
Contrapuntals and just enjoy the pop of drops on
Concrete and leaf, birdfeeder, wind-chime, brick
And toppled bucket. The sharp tang of ozone
Invigorated-*rain-smell what a blessing rain-smell!*

Some phoebe, bluebird or sparrow, digging on the
Program, would go ahead and add a few cheeps and
Trills from the trees, their efforts near-obliterated by the constant,
Hissing spatter and drum-thrum of winter's icy inveigh.
They tried, they tried, tried throughout the morning
And afternoon. Like the Farmers Market folks braving
The rain to pitch their sunshades in the parking-lot
Outside the SOCO and OC Mix down the road.
Wedges of Canadian geese would pass overhead,
Honking loud as pitchmen at a summer fair's Product
Parade. *They tried, they tried, tried* throughout the
Morning and afternoon-to add something sweet to
Warm the gelid creep in the cakewalks and contrapuntals

 Todd French

Of the cold season's wet and weare.

There was music inside the house: my wife Maureen,
Pushed back at the day's preternatural dark and the drag
Of her nascent cold, with the aid of her cherished
Concertina-which she has been dragging out of the
Closet these last few weekends. The instrument looks
Much like an accordion and its body shaded the brown
And black of beech bough and oak trunk-the hue of a
Chocolate pitbull or lab, a mourning cloak or a
Horace Duskywing. The grips were the color of burnt
Umber or ancient nutmeg. For the life of me, I could
Not remember the occasion when Mo had purchased it,

When she first started practicing with it.

And she started playing.

And we forgot the rain.

And just like that the day's dark and damp disappeared:
The sibilance of shower fall reduced to background
Of swollen brook chuckle. It was mead and malt for the ear;
It was hot tea for the tympanum and it filled the house
With its delightful wheezes, chuffs, shrills and shucks
Of aural delight. There was no cold except the one that
She was fighting. As Mo worked the concertina, its
Body pleated as an oriental fan or a date palm's fronds,
My spirit glowed-the internal works brightened like
Prince Johnathan's eyes when he consumed the honey
That dripped from the tip of his walking-stick in that
Beautiful pause in mortal alarums against Philistine arms.
The house was full of music. The kids dug it and so did I.

The sun came out.

It was as if the season-for a nonce-had kicked off its galoshes
For a pair of sandals or crocs (the moment she started playing),

As if April had just blasted by in a Corvette of turquoise green,
And a young girl, ponytail flying, dark glasses flaring with sundogs,
Had tossed us a bottle of Dandelion or Rosemary Wine in passing.
For a while, I felt the blowtorch touch of an early spring:
Fresh-cut grass, airborne glyphs writ with petal and seed;
Springtime's hot, blowsy breath on coast mustard and
Bush sunflower and thistle-on meadow and glade's riot-shot of
Goldenrod, California poppy; hillsides fuzzed with the
Red and orange foundry spill of Devil's Paintbrushes,
Wildflowers-rippling, zig-zagging chains of Shasta daisies
With egg-yolk centers running up to rises of blue oak and
California buckeye. You could hear it all in: treble, treble
Tenor, baritone, bass-with every open and close of the
Bellows-happiness flew like blindingly beautiful quetzals
From room to room.

I wanted to plait a crown of bluebells for my wife in appreciation
Of the gift.

And when the music slowed

The long emphysema gulps and gusts of aureate gold made you
Imagine old men remembering friends, arguments and
Lost loves as they battled over checkers and chess on
Indian Summer days in the park.

Eventually, Mo put down her concertina and the rain
Renewed its sonorous tracks.

Quietude reigned.

The twins worked on some art projects or read.

Gwen perused a new book.

Everyone was content.

Once in a while I drifted up to the kitchen window

 TODD FRENCH

With a sweating mug in hand, to catch a glimpse
Of a couple hummingbirds zipping past the bedraggled
Japanese privet tree-their too-tight jackets of acrylic green
Reduced to a dusty cactus shade by the screen of precipitation.

The house had been full of music.

And it had been a joy to hear it.

PERSONAL PSALM/01/22/24

Imprecatory Psalm Against the WEF.

Who are you, you half-men-half-gods of the WEF,
That you should scorn the Lord and curse His Anointed,
And say, neither the dragnet nor the fowler will they send
Against us-all the earth and its fulness belong to us, for we
Have taken council against all the families of the earth,
And will pen them-hedge them in like the market deer in spring!
Ah, you mean and women boasting of your wealth and seared
Consciences: you have said in the darkness of your benighted souls,
God neither hears, or does good or ill: He will do nothing on behalf
Of His saints when the stars of the restraining nations are flung
To earth and their constitutions and laws dispersed as harvest chaff;
The Lord does not live. Who can gainsay our claim to dominion?
In the pride of your hearts you have said, there is no help
In their God: we are *gods* and the staff and the rod is
In our hands; we are gods and we will exalt our horn and make
An end to those who put their trust in the Lord!

Foolish men and women! The Lord lives! The heavens
And the earth and all therein belong to The Holy One of Israel!
He has made for Him an everlasting throne and kingdom;
There will be no end to His reign when He returns with
His army of saints. The Profane Ones in Davos who have said
We will take away all the possessions of the people,
And we will give them the filth of the earth to feed their children,
They will not boast to the one who knows what they are about,

The One who confounds the councils of men: He will not forget them
On the day He goes forth to fight against His enemies like
A man of valor. Though they growl like the bears and the young
Bears, He will end the Time of Offense and slough off the
Skin of the old earth they have sworn to remake.
He will send a storm upon them when they have said:
There will be no storms and the heat will not oppress those
Who have made their agreement with us. God will break them
As a skilled hunter breaks the eye-teeth of the lion.
Neither their plans or denial of God will stand: they will all
Wear away like a banner in a winter gale: no one will remember
Their names when God has made an end of them.

Be instructed while there is time, you false gods of the WEF:

Put your faith in the Ancient One of Days who placed the
Garland of Crowns in the heavens and laid down the foundations
Of the world with The Word. He humbles the kings and the captains,
And He lifts the poor from the earth and gives them a hope and a
Living. He made a nation of a small people when they were
Without land and He gave an inheritance to the handmaiden and
Her child when they languished; He uplifted Judges and Kings,
And blessed and rebuked them when He desired. He shows mercy
To the merciful and destroys the council of the wicked. His apostles
And ministers have proclaimed The Way to the children of men.
You lawless men know that God lives-it is in the hearts of men
And women to have a knowledge of God. Why do you spurn
Righteousness and holiness to make a tumult in the earth's waning days?
None of your kingdoms will stand-they will fly like the sand from
The dune's crest in the wind-vanish like the sea-spume against the
Headland. You are no more than the short-horned locusts who swarm
And are driven away by the smoke of the pits. You can do no more
Than the Lord decrees and though you rise in your eyes as the
Hollyhocks in summer, He will utterly make an end of you in His time.

But those who have put their trust in God will have a sure inheritance
And a living hope: they are under the grace and they have been gifted
With salvation. God is a present help to those who fear and extol Him,

And are not ashamed of the gospel of everlasting life. When they share
The words of Truth, their report is sweeter than Acacia honey in the
Ears of the Lord-their fame runs like the springboks and cheetahs
Before the Throne. The humble and contrite remember the commandments
Of the Son: to show the world how they can be saved by belief in the
Lamb who takes away the sins of the world. They do not fear the
Wrath of man-of the great ones of renown who have set themselves against
The Lord and His Anointed: they are resolved on the saving of many,
To spread the Good News to those apportioned to hear and believe.
God is a buckler and shield to those who believe on Him and He revives
Them in the night watches and restores them in the reveille of morning's
Light-he renews and strengthens them when they stumble or doubt.
There is no limit to the undeserved mercies and loving kindness of God:
Go and count the awns of the wheat spike if you would lay them for account.

But the wicked will fall before Him like the Philistines before the sword
Of Shammah when he took his stand in the lentil field.

DOG AND SWAN

For Klaus Schwab and the Rest of The WEF at Davos

I know, I know: I am part of the colonizing, anti-Green, imperializing,
Genocidal, white, patriarchal, selfish carbon-footprint that needs to go,
Shuffle off to Buffalo (do people still shuffle off to Buffalo), take a hike,
Go into the ze *pitchen darken* at the behest of Gaia. We're just all-well
Not all-a bunch of penny Phaetons looking for a Chariot of The Sun, yes?
But it's like this and please bear with me as I elucidate my state of thought:
You know how someone is walking their flame-colored golden retriever
Black, labrador or silver bull by the park lake's edge? Let's say it's early
Morning when dawn's caul of pearlescent light is being burned away
By the big, flayed ball of the sun, and that's when our dog-owner

Ah…yes, I am sorry I said *dog*.

Yes, yes, that's true: one day warm-blooded pets like dogs and cats
Will be prohibited and we'll all be happy with a giant Madagascar centipede
Named Romulus.

Bear with me, but *I want no bears with me.*

And then, that dog looks up as its nosing its way down the shore,
Maybe hoping for a nice fat squirrel or rabbit to chase and harry,
And it catches sight of an infuriatingly beautiful brace of
Swans gliding smoothly across the mirror surface of the water,
And-yep-the animal rips its leash out of its master's hand and barking
Fit to kill, it hits the shallows with a righteous *whump* and is ploughing its
Way to the prey, scattering the sleepy coots, geese, mallards, bluegill
And crappies. Fair enough: that's the way that endearing beast's mind
Is hardwired-it wants The Swans. And as you watch the bowwow
(pardon the pun) doggedly paddling toward the unattainable objective, head
Jerking and jiggling, chuffing and huffing, black tongue lolling to the side of
Its mouth, fighting for every bit of progress through the brackish moil,
And maybe the doggie doesn't want a Swan Burger (hold the mayo),
Or tapping into its long-buried Birder genetic make-up-but, hear me out,
Maybe it's about the inexpressible animal grasp of Life, Joy and Objectives:
Slipping the leash and hitting the water with a big belly-flop, paws splayed,
Wind whistling through the fur-and man, those swans are taking themselves
Soooooo seriously, someone's got to shock them out of their avian
Self-regard, so-Dog and Bird/Dog and Swan-canine torpedo seeking
The Unbeatable Foe-fun, fun, fun!

You just know that as soon as the canine gets within a decent distance of
Those birds which have been majestically changing course with the
Measured grace of an antebellum miss avoiding a bad dance partner,
Wings touched with the sun's peach and scarlet fire, *you know*, they are going
To lift from the water with perfect timing, speed and aplomb, taking to the air
To light down somewhere on the other side. And unphased, the dog will
Correct course and go after them even as the owner is yelling and cursing
Man's Best Friend to give up the quest and get out of the water. He knows
That now there has to be a bath *for this bath*. Maybe in its doggy brain, the dog
Realizes it's *never* going to catch these snooty birds with pinions pristine as
Sir Lohengrin's knightly crest, it is going to swim until it wears itself out and
Sheepishly heads back to shore and its less-than-happy owner. Any lake bird
Is just going to keep flying and lighting down, or leave the lake altogether
And plop down in some other part of the park.

　　　　　TODD FRENCH

But the dog is having a wonderful time whether it gets a swan or not. It's having a *whale* of a time.

The unabashed brio of Life-Chase-Movement-Play-Light-Water-Joy.

The dog has to *try* to get the swan.

It just *has to.*

It's the same for me and my family, Mr. Schwab, and many, many others.

We *have to try to live.*

We *have to.*

We love the process/mystery/joy/preciousness of Life.

There's always something new.

Dog and Swan, you know?

God has made us that way.

WAVES

Come day's end, stand on a coast bluff, or the end of a pier,
And watch the waves come rolling in-the dark green of
Bat Flower or Bracken Ferns-green-black of a helmet's combat-ivy,
Lightly dusted with the rusty carmine blush of sunset and
Threaded here and there with the ocean's needlework of
Kelp and sea grass. Take a moment to lean into the chill
Wind's insistent tug and contemplate the endless come of comber
And breaker smashing against rock and sand, tide's retreat,
Tide's return. Listen to the sough, sigh and thunder of water and
Salt-take it all in-the rise and fall of the deep's heart-song,
The *voice of the waters* unconquered (*until Shiloh come*),
Resonant and restless, humbling-feel the pull, the
Soul's soar and souls ebb worked out in awe and wonder

And you can imagine:

The empyrean waves of never-ending praise from angelic
Lips-the eternal lyre and kinnor-strum of spirit's palate
Of those attendant souls gathered around the rainbow-girded
Throne where The Ancient One of Days-blazing in jasper and
Carnelian's cast receives the *glory, glory, glory* that comes
Unceasing to divinity's ears. Consider line after line of
Curling surf's wind-whipped hoods rearing up to fall on
Beach shingle and you can picture the four figures surrounding
The seat of God-winged and bearing the faces of Man, Lion,
Ox, Eagle-praising without pause, without let-up; granted
The gift of lucency's eternal leitmotif: My God, all honor and

     TODD FRENCH

Glory goes to You: did You not say that even the things
Of the deep would declare Your glory-whale and bream,
Nautilus and narwhale-why shouldn't the deep declare
Your glory-unceasing, unstinting, day in and day out?
Why shouldn't we hear the celestial lap and drub of
Cherubim and Seraphim's lingua against the throne from
Which living waters will one day run?

When I watch the waves rush toward shore in the last
Embers of the afternoon's light-the endless motion of
Liquid and mass-hear the sound of seawater's slam over
And over, it isn't hard to form an image of the heavenly choir
Exulting in its endless, loving program, to hear the words

Of truth that could sunder mountains and birth nebulae:
Offered up to You, *Elohim.*

"Holy, holy, holy, is the Lord God Almighty,
who was and is and is to come!"

"Worthy are you, our Lord and God,
to receive glory and honor and power,
for you created all things,
and by your will they existed and were created."

WINTER CLOUD

I see
A chef
His tall hat
Falling from his head
As he kneels down
To pray

WINTER STORM/02/05/24

Standing in front of the kitchen window watching the glass'
Blur of wet squall and bedraggled green, I am suddenly seized by
The memory of bathing my baby girls in the sink, sure that,
Slippery as fresh-bought mackerel or trout, they would fly
Out of my hands, executing impromptu, hazardous helicals
And bi-plane whorls inches beneath the ceiling-fizzing out like
Deflating balloons, banking against the walls and furniture
Before coming to rest, bruised and shrieking, somewhere
Near the living room fireplace.

ANGELFOOD DONUTS N-SUCH/02/19/24

Despite the rain and wind blowing through
The donut shop's open doorway, the snarling leopard
On the young counter lady's white Def Leppard sweatshirt

Surprises a smile from me.

MANZIKERT/ROMANUS IV DIOGENES

The **Battle of Manzikert** or **Malazgirt** was fought between the Byzantine Empire and the Seljuk Empire on 26 August 1071[9] near Manzikert, theme of Iberia (modern Malazgirt in Muş Province, Turkey). The decisive defeat of the Byzantine army and the capture of the Emperor Romanos IV Diogenes[10] played an important role in undermining Byzantine authority in Anatolia and Armenia,[11] and allowed for the gradual Turkification of Anatolia. Many Turks, travelling westward during the 11th century, saw the victory at Manzikert as an entrance to Asia Minor.[12] (Wikipedia).

When the emperor Romanus IV Diogenes was removed from the throne following the catastrophic defeat of the Byzantine forces in Manzikert, he was blinded, the blinding as brutal as possible, loaded on to a donkey and conveyed to a monastery at Ponti, where he soon died of his injuries.

Tied to the ass, that jogged and jounced, battered him in the saddle,
Empty sockets black with flies and infection, head which bore the diadem's
Cross, the gold, gems and pearls-the images of the apostles-now a
Seething cap of worms and maggots-what went through his mind as fever and trauma
Flung his life back and forth like a polo ball by horsemen in the Hippodrome?
His enemy, the malicious monk, historian and courtier Michael Psellos could
Not resist getting some last licks in, congratulating him on his blindness,
Because surely the Lord intended him to receive a higher light in the aftermath.
Betrayed on the battlefield by Andronicus Ducas who led the reserves, he had
Fought valiantly until Sultan Alp Arslan's Turks had overcome his broken forces.
Now, in the throes of his pain, the whistling arrow-arc of agony pure as the ecstasy of
A column-bound religious stylus, wide as the cerulean canopy of sky on
The Terrible Day, did the emperor pray for death as Jonah when the gourd dried,

Curse the fickleness of the Roman people to their rulers-their intrigues, the
Palace revolutions and seditions, the banished shed of eyes and genitals as
Summer's unripe figs or autumn's laurel leaves? Did the emperor, called to
The Purple by Constantine's widow to defeat the Turkish incursions and reconcile
The state bureaucracy and military (impossible! Can the lion and the leveret
Produce an issue?), reflect in the interstice between fever and infection's
Cressets blazing in his head and lungs upon King Josiah, the *basileus* of Judah
Who dis so much good before falling in a fight that God forbade him to join?
Did he hear-in pain-wracked gobbets-the words of King David when news
Was brought him of Saul's suicide before the Philistine host-how the mighty
Are fallen in the midst of battle, the words as comforting as a cold wind caroming
Off a campaign tent's canvas

As the donkey stumbled, listed, throwing him back and forth across the filthy
Flea-covered blankets, the sniggers, jeers and insults of his escort battering his
Ears like the somnolent quorking of Anatolia's buzzards, the occasional swat
From an open hand or fist against the side of his vermin-ravaged skull, the flies the heat
The flies the heat would there never be an end to the flies buzzing lighting buzzing
Perhaps the Higher Light touted by the cruel Psellus was already at work in
The criminally abused sockets and reeling mind-the

But the Lesser Light

The Lesser Light

Enabled

Made Able

Light's refraction/focused on retina/visual spectrum's conversion into electrical
Impulses by rods and cones/retina's glean to optic nerve to brain to process
The image leading to sight/light striking retina beginning the visual processing

That had to be at work-sputtering, winking in the abused holes the gore-rimmed
Rabbit-holes through which the frisking Turkish horsemen made their false retreats,
Shaggy pony's ass-tail show sweat-soaked quarters discernable through dust-screen:
How often did that play out in his mind and residue of sight's dried jelly Andronicus'
Defection/labarum falling/sun raking/fishy bait-ball shellac of lamellar armor under

Sun/sun/no respite from sun/dust/blood-stink/horse-stink/this is Rome this is Rome,
How can these barbarians best us/how can this be army death army death/Alp Arlsan's
Deal spurned/army death/Taken/taken/Sultan's foot on his neck face in the death
After being taken one of the surviving Varangians vomiting blood another trying
To remake his belly/the arrows the arrows after the damn Turks turn

Here I am in the Turk's tent with a boot on my neck

Here I am stroking the cheek of a jewel-festooned empress, her coal-dark eyes
Lambent and unfocused as she says *you will make a wonderful step-father to my
Michael* and the soft dune of her breast in my hand then raised up in the Hippodrome
On golden shields acclaimed Romanus IV lion-pit of Ducates and Comnenas lion-pit
Never ends plot complot counter-plot Treasury Party Army Party allegiance no more
Than a scum of crumbs on a fish-pond's surface incense and ceremony liturgy
Gold throne gold incense and ceremony liturgy's angel-tongue exaltation
Ah one general after another taking The Purple remember what Tzimices did to
Nicephorus leaving him mangled on his ascetic's leopard-skin cloak always
Someone Ducates and Comnenas lion-pit lion-pit always squabbling and no end

Of Turks Pechengs Bulgars Russe and she spread beneath me hair fanned out
On the pillow opening opening for me and everything given the world the world
The sight of the torturer's face the sweaty pores the sickle of a scar on the forehead
And pain no heated iron eye gouge then dark dark screaming and fainting and
There is the boot of a Turkish sultan on my neck and my face is down on the tent
Carpet thread and dirt a blur before eyes I still had eyes had eyes my God how can it
Come to this clash of chains torturer leaning forward fingers hooked rub out the
Mind's light let me die on the way to the monastery let me die

I see my mother bending over with a spoon of gruel in the morning's ghost-light
Her eyes tired but her voice is kind

Eyes gone/donkey jounce/donkey-bounce/sun-broil/worm-moil/fly-toil

Never see women soldiers crown throne children birds animals clergy vestments
Dream of light-stream in Hagia Sophia blue sky rain robe silk battle standards
Horses olives dates melons flowers oh flowers never see never see sea the
vsea a baby reaching for its mother's arms breast the down on her arms I held her in
my arms saw the flecks of

Gold in her soft brown eyes the strings of crown-pearls the jewels of her crown cast
In candle-light gold-red as I bend to kiss her take her take it all all there for the taking
Cheers of excubitors scholarae Varangians thema troopers all there for the taking
Michael to be set aside later just these Turks these Turks to pursue to the end of the world
The end of the world

Oh God oh God take memory with sight brick up the little holes that discern and still
See they see they see they see they see they see

Someone hits me on the right cheek and the rest laugh as I reel in the saddle

I was a Basileus
I was a Basileus
How can I be nothing
Oh God how can I be nothing
How can it be nothing like God stealing ten tribes
From Solomon's son
How can I be nothing

LIVING AGAIN

One day God will grant an antidote for grief, a provision for
Suffering. I can't tell you when. But sometime, when you are
Sitting on your stoop, half-awake, gaze glazed, the grit of
Earth beneath the ragged half-moons of your nails, the
Grave-side sour of pomegranate on your tongue, it will sneak
Up on you, like a tortoiseshell cat coming up on your blindside
To rub its head beneath your chin-reacquainting you with the
Purring lingua of life, light and hope. It will take time for the heart
And head to trade out cold cabbage soup for hot posole;
There's no set date, no calendar's check-sorrows do not abide by
Seasons, star-charts or almanacs: we give up the comfort of
Crow fairs and autumn quays when months, years and mending
Effect their work, whether it's through Scripture's balm,
New love's gain, the affection of a rescue terrier, the discipline
Of dance, origami or the archer's art-the soul warms again
When it wills. That might be little solace when we stumble
Through hours blindly like lost spelunkers navigating by
Stalagmites' phosphorus-but eventually, we see our way
Out of the dark and reaffirm our bond with the difficult task
Of *going on*. We aren't Tristan, waiting for Isolde to sign
A healing with a white sail on the horizon-but in time,
Broken hearts are repaired in a fashion, and we *go on*.
And honey and cinnamon replaces the taste of pomegranate.

We go on because there's no recourse.

We love again because we can do no less.

DEVOTION POEM/ANGLO-SAXON STYLE

Go up with God's help against the opposer's bone-locks,
Bent against you in the war-sweat won in spirit's battle,
Break the shining ship-moon riveted to the foe-shoulder,
Shatter the meat-makers shimmied from the thigh-sheaths;
Without God's aid, workers of waves can vanquish a prince,
With heart-cares and hurly batter at his boat-drake,
Before he finds the shore where surety of friends awaits.
Do not look to loft the Lindworm of battle-light alone,
When the soul is tried by the trials of a troop's tide.
Call upon the Christ then-do not count it craven:
Hold to the High one who hung above the Cross Hill,
He hears the precious prayers of all-thane, thrall or earl.
Give glory to the river-gold gleaned from the Gospels,
Better than gold mail or scale of *Miklgard*;
The words of Life are sharp, like winter-shine of war worm,
They can carry Man through the currents of cruel cuts.
Brief is breath and valor bound within the bone-house,
Trust cannot be tallied in the stoutness of the steel.
Turn to the Name whose kindle shames the sky's candle;
Jesus helms the just who have chosen to live for faith.

Woden did not deign to wear the bitter tree's beam,
To win men's souls from the pits of Hell's perils;
It was the Galilean who briefly gave the ghost up,
To make the children of men richer than a land-winner.
It is the Son who comforts the bereft and broken-hearted,
He, with a hawk's pinion, shields the dreamers in the dust,

Lifts up the snow's leman, who sells her body for its savor,
He knows our sorrows, His were heavier than a boar's helm!
Do not err and call the Christian's share a sheep-faith,
To think them no account, like the worst of cattle-kin.
In weakness His war-men are stronger than a brace of bear-shirts,
Wiser than the thinkers who spend the spray of Kvasir's spittle,
In the writings of Apostles, the play of Life is pointed out!
I read those words, when night breached my deck with breakers,
My wave-speaker no more than the auger of the auk's cry,
My cheerful sounder, the caustic skirls of gull and cormorant.
The winds took my bone-warmth as I clave to the keel's groove,
But the psalms of the Scope-King, saved me in the deep swells
The words of the Lord's skald, they arrowed me along!

The warrior of the God-way, remembers The Resurrection,
Every day without fear of the threat of flame's farewell,
He knits a ring-coat from the sounds of the Son's runes,
Set down by the seekers, given to the Mystery of Grace.
He does not fear, weapon-weather or moil of billow maidens,
His sea-steed is safe from the breaker of trees.
How many chieftains have died-ground down with beard's gray,
Their byrnies bundled up; rings red as the feuce of fox fur?
Few have known the shade-fall of what they call the bed-shame,
To die in the peace-mizzle that Christ showers on the meek.
Who are the earth-shakers who mock the Son of Man,
And give little regard for the hope in heaven's heir?
Many with a name have hacked themselves a hearth-hall,
Only to see their world-egg burnt down to alder's ash.
Carls have seen their ax arm fail within the deep fray,
Kings have leapt the ship's gunnel into the whale-road's weft.
Bad winds blow when the whelm of wealth and might comes,
When the cloak of new scarlet is shared out to the shoulder,
When the graven cup of mind's-mead, is given after battle.
All the things of earth end like the drizzled dew of evening,
And plenty goes the way of paint upon the shield's-shoal.
I have seen the Russe and Northmen, garbed in the Greek King's gold,
Beggared in days like storm-blossoms stripped from the beech;

But those who call upon Christ, they have the high hedge,
They have life Everlasting, beyond the thin spring of their span;
I have not seen the righteous begging for the alms of armlets,
I have not seen their bread bowls wasted by want.

Put your trust in the One who defeated the Death-Tree,
Reckon the sail-road that leads through Him to salvation.

TODD FRENCH

JUST BEFORE DAWN

Restless, we wake when the pre-dawn dark pushes at the panes,
Like some animal eager for the draughts and drams of the People Lights,
And make out way to the kitchen, microwaving a cup of coffee
As black as the River Ruki or the dreams of anglerfish.
It doesn't matter: something calls us-like leaf-ripple of the
Summer aspens, or the whisper/card-fan flutter of the wings
Of a bird caught in the chimney. Does it matter why we wake:
To suffer sleep-grit, the stagger through the unheated hall,
To cold linoleum beneath the heals in order to sit down and
Peruse the eternal truths of the gospels-psalms, proverbs,
Admonitions of prophets and calls to repentance?
Whatever compels us-a dream of a single red rose
Blazing blue from a snowbank-or the fading laughter of a
Family reunion (not your own) in some unidentifiable
Central European country-it doesn't matter what tossed you
Out of bed in the early hours to sit, cooling caffeine at hand,
To open the book and peruse the word.

And then the cold and pre-morning twilight is forgotten,
And the heart/mind/spirit warms like the candescence of
A new soul woven into a womb-or a fresh star emerging from
Dust and gas' dance out of some quadrant's molecular cloud as you
Reacquaint yourself with the God-Life-Love-breathed words
Of The Son who could look down from the cross into the
Faces of the mob breathing Calvary hill's alkali-bitter pollen
Of hate and derision and entreat The Father:

"Forgive them Father: they know not what they do."

Read them, and all the world's horrors dissipate
Like squid's ink in sun-strafed seawater as we remind ourselves
That such love such forgiveness such salvation and redemption
Exists and our sins are covered-our entry to The Kingdom secured;
That there is a saving/succor for the fallen on this globe.
As a dream of a blue or red rose sprouting from a snowbank,
At the end of the lane of the old country's deciduous woods we forget
Atrocities-barbarism vivid as the blue glaze of Berlin's Ishtar Gate.
The words of Life and Love from The Son of Man suffice,
It contents us, even as dawn's pewter starts to sketch the
Backyard in broad strokes before the morning's wash of
Orange and red spinels buff their lusters.
"Forgive them Father: they know not what they do."

TODD FRENCH

HOUR OF THE WOLF

It is that hour when more people wrapped in the whelm of dreams
Feel the brief impress of the toe-tag brushing the metatarsal,
The quick touch of mortality's pass.

It is the hour, the restless hour black as an Aztec's
Obsidian Macuahuitl, black as whale oil, when you are up,
And memory and conscience are having it out in their
Sunless corrida and you into shuffle into the kitchen to heat up
Old coffee, the linoleum under your soles cold as
An early frost, cold as the death-spread swiped like jam
Between old stars.

It is the hour when you sit down, rubbing sleep's grit
From your eye and *something* passes over you like
Peter's shadow over the hopeful lame and you open
Your heart to God in that pitch-black interstice
Broken by kitchen's jaundice-jump of florescence,
The contented snoring from family in other parts of
The House

And

The soul opens opens like the night-blooming cereus,
Four O'Clocks or moonflowers

And you say, *God, God, can we talk a while?*

SPRING

DANDELIONS

Before we leave for the mall, my daughter Victoria insists
On executing her (absent) mom's mission as a Dandelion Slayer.
She ranges across the lawn, stooping to decapitate the sun-wigged
Weeds with aplomb, as if they were jolly jacqueries of some
Failed (Nature) revolution deserving nothing but the edge of the
Guillotine's blade, or a surge of insurgents making their way
Through the green undulant waves of the enemy's lines.
Before we head out, my daughter (to her twin's consternation)
Insists on wiping out a good handful or two.

No mercy to be had here.

Like mother, like daughter.

Perhaps all girls, all women are born to be cold-hearted
Killers of dandelions.

On occasion, I remind my wife that in massive properties,
Dandelions are gifted with cancer-fighting properties and then
She reminds me that thousands of dandelions would have to be
Culled to make it worth it and I would probably have to buy her
A massive new colander to assay the task and who knows to what
Degree the medicinal boost will kick in?

As I watch Victoria slaughter the dandies with focus and determination,
I recall Charles Schultz's Charlie Brown lying supine on his pitcher's
Mound, rooked by a fastball, his head enswathed by the weeds, finding

TODD FRENCH

For a moment, before the next blazing swat, a kind of peace amidst the
Golden flowers.
And I think of the ghosts of Ray Bradbury's Green Town Illinois residents
Watching Victoria waste this particular crop, shaking their heads in
Mock sorrow, saying:

That might have made a sweet bottle of summer wine.

SONG

Be grateful to God for the days of peace,
For hours as bright and smooth as Cretan sea-glass.
Behold the lands reeling like drunkards towards war,
Mouthing minotaur credos, huffing like bulls of Bashan.

Fortunate the men and women whose children
Have never heard the klaxons of Bomb-Shelter Time.

ORCHARD

Let's throw our Mackintoshes, Opals, Grannies, Honeycrisps and Galas
At one another and give chase-brash as jangled teens-through
Our respective orchards-the fruit-laden limbs and branches stark
Against a captivating murex shell bleed of twilight's purple,
While the crows, feathers blade-sharp and dusty as anthracite,
Take to the air, complaining as they always do in their
Tobacco chaw-cheeked dug-out blather, that anyone should have
An iota of fun-ah, who needs those killjoys-off with them!
I want to talk sweet section, quarter, cider and seed to you
As I pursue you through the narrow rows, kicking aside the windfalls,
My fingers grazing the back of your sweater as your sweet laughter,
Chimes, caroms and ricochets off each precious, sugary orb above our heads,
Your dark hair streaming-black as jet or black tiger eye sapphires,
Black as tourmalines about your throat picked out by candle flair,
Your unshod feet green with grass stains, your shoes buried back
Behind us in a bushel basket of red Fujis. I long to see you dancing
From trunk to trunk-daring me to catch you on the next pass.
The dark comes too early and the coddling moth and plum curculios
Will have their way with the brief sweets dangling above: let us
Try to remember the first days when love's volition was assured.

Like Appollo gaining ground on Daphne or impalas and elands in courtship,
I want us to play in Orchard Time as we did in autumns past when we had
The speed, the thrum and stretch of tendon, muscle-the reality of
Of ligament's largesse-the sight of you/self of you reaffirming it all.
Age inveighs; but I would we be drunk upon one another, our mouths
Refreshed by the vintage of heritage or Golden Russet-let the dipper

Have its concupiscence with the barrel. Yes, let us remember the love
We evinced from the beginning. I want to celebrate us: leaf, stem, seeds,
Core, flesh-from the early days when the root called to row, rain to the earth.
I still love you: like Isaac in the fields, thought-lost before he heard
The first approach of his Rebekkah. I would run after you now,
Scattering the rabbits, mice, towhees and starlings from the fields.
Against the stunning murex shell bleed of twilight's Tyrian purple,
I would take you in my arms and whisper: "let us joy our orchards,"
In spite of the short days and cold blows, sun's weak silver nitrate
Shine-I would talk section, quarter, cider and seed to you.

Let us throw our Mackintoshes, Opals, Grannies, Honeycrisps and Galas

At one another and give chase-brash as jangled teens-through our respective
Orchards-let mine join yours and yours join mine. Let us be a fruitful field,
A harvest fiddle's sizzle winding its way from trunk to crown.

I want to chase you to a decent knoll, the grass, a leaning
Sea blazoned *vert and undy* and watch you take the rungs
Set in the dark bark-scooting you way up, heart light as eider,
And I want to climb up after you-the years gone,
And look up your skirt-watching it open and bell like
The campanulas and kaffir lilies.

FIRST KISS

Sunfire/equator blaze/lava plume/lightning strike to terebinth's knot

Molten bird molting in the heart's cage

The moment your lips touched hers

RABBIT EARS

It won't happen on my block though the big municipal park
Is just across the street from our turn-in and we are gifted
With the odd wild/semi-wild visitor-squirrels scrambling on the backwall,
Running across the roof, darting through the maze of branches
Of our neighbor's willow, ungainly possums stumping from hedge
To hedge and the very, very occasional raccoon high-tailing it
From the garbage cans between the houses back to Mile Square Park
Ringed tail insouciantly upraised like a false flag of surrender

Even so I would love it if God would swing it

That I could get up early one morning when everyone's asleep
Open the front door, pad silently down the concrete walkway

And see

The Bahama conch pink of the sun's first rays
Setting afire the veins in the long pricked ears
Of a fat jackrabbit or study desert hare
Sitting on his haunches
In the middle of my front lawn

FAITH

¹⁵ so that they even carried out the sick into the streets and laid them on cots and mats, that as Peter came by at least his shadow might fall on some of them.

Acts 5:15
English Standard Version

Imagine that: to have such faith in God's healing powers that you,
The fevered, broken mendicant, the lock-limbed patient would
Say, lay my bed on the cobblestones, in the dust for I know that
If Peter's shadow passes, if but a fraction of a head, an arm, a
Tattered dip-swing of robe should overflow me, I will be spelled
From bone break and bad blood-as a runner catching his breath
Beneath the blue/sun/breeze scatter of acacia and cedar shade;
I will be as a man or woman basking on a blanket, banded by
Moonshine breathed out by the carob's limbs, the song of the
Fire-fronted Serin joined to my blood-I will be the carob
Stretching my arms and legs-whole whole-whole-bone and
Muscle strumming like kinnor strings like a yew harp with
Gratitude-I will be the rock bunting singing and winging
Paying tribute to the loving kindnesses of the Most High;
I will be the runner Ahimaaz that outpaced the Cushite to
Give King David the battle news. I will be as the river's arm
That overleaps the bank to flood the first blue and white flowers
Of spring, that plunges down into the burrow of the spadefoot toad;
I will be a single bead of salt water riding the pinion of a sea eagle
Soaring upwards to lay a kiss on heaven's solar disk.
I will be a hoof on the Persian fallow deer as it skips through the green

And I will canter in colt-time in joy in gratitude in worship.

Lord: let Peter's shadow touch me and I will walk.

Lord: let Peter's shadow pass over me and I will run.

*Song of sandal and breath's ratchet, I will run and I will praise
You forever.*

MEDIEVAL GERMAN MINNESONG

When the storm blew, we tied our horses to the beech trees,
And we took our ease beneath its limbs, waiting for calm,
While the wind sent the yellow-green flowers spinning,
Catching in your tresses-those wild chestnut-colored streamers,
Which whipped about your fair cheeks and brow like a brace
Of new pennons unfolded at a landgrave's tilt. Those asters,
Bled by the beeches well-suited your locks better than a
Circlet of white gold! Beneath the sickles of your brows,
Your moth-green eyes shone with the fawn-hued light of
April-the dark little cuts in their glass catching the sun's
Blown stipple: I wanted to be forever baptized in their
Depths-to rise each morning and wade into the font and
Jordan of their gaze. When I took you in my arms beneath
The tangled arms of the beeches, my heart leapt like a
Tower hawk from the wrist!

As the sheep-puffs of cloud were carried along in their herds
On their meadows and meads of dazzling blue-their wool,
White and gray, blasted by the billows, I turned you,
Your lips parting, your green eyes half-shuttered, still
Jiggling in their sockets with mirth, and brought my mouth
To yours. Your plush lips were as sweet as an unhalved apple
At first bite, softer than the stole of a bishop on Easter Day.
You trembled in my arms like a morning-new lamb or
Thrush from the shell. Beneath your yellow surcoat,
The hillocks of your breasts pressed against me while the
Beech trees, in approval of our *amour*, crowned us with

Their blossoms-their limbs clashed in tribute even as
Our steeds whinnied in the blue shadow and dapple.
The sword on my belt, wrapped in blue-stained leather,
Bearing its rows of gilded scallop shells, danced like a lute
In the hands of a castle-singer; the wind-shivered sun
Made the lapis stone on my hilt glow like a sea-swell at noon.

We did not think about the wind's shocks as we stood in
The shelter of the trees on the edge of that little grove,
When our lips met-we didn't mind the rattle-gabble and
Jingle of horse-harness and the slam of my small shield
Against the saddle-bow-ah, how those three eagles of white
On blue wanted to take flight-we knew the bliss of the

Higher Ones! The curve of your body was fair as the bow
Of Ulysses when he strung it against the impious suitors
Of Penelope. My heart's tambour joyed to meet your own
As we pressed against one another beneath the branches
That dipped and rose as the war-beaks on the bows of the
Ships of the Kaiser of Sicily. There was no time, no meaning,
There amidst the hurly of the green-the blue and red flowers
Mashed at our feet when I held you, the maiden of my heart,
The one whose soul is as pure as the argent heron, within
The circle of my arms. I thanked my Savior and all the
Evangelists for the miracle of your precious *self.* I counted
The gold rings, cups and myrtle-caps won with lance and
Sword as *nothing* when I took that kiss when we paused from
Our ride. I would have counted the Orphan Stone of the
Kaiser's crown as nothing compared to the savor of those
Small inches of delightful skin.

When we broke our embrace, the little sparrows and thrushes
Who fought the whorls and whacks of the storm to hold their place
Upon the air sang twice as loud-it seemed to me-as if they were
Happy to see us take our ease, and the broken beams carved thin
As ash staves blazed with thrice the season's surfeit of fawn-light.
When you leaned your head upon my shoulder's fold of flaring
Cloak, your smile curving into its pigeon-gray, your breath

        TODD FRENCH

Sweet as the bees' comb-I was content, and could have gone from
This world up to The Maker's seat, to merry plead your merits
Before that august tribunal. As you leaned into me, the warmth of
Your hips pressed into mine, I did not feel the pain of the old wounds
Won in the Prussian lands, where the idols sprout like those of
Bel and Nebo in Old Babylon. I made for another kiss, but you
Shook your head, eyes downcast, biting your lower lip, before
You said *we should go back* and that you would make a favor
Of your sleeve studded with garnets and bequeath it to me before
I was yare for the next tilt in the lists. So, we left off our tender
Ministrations, with naught but the birds and red squirrels and
Our horses to witness our love.

You told me as I held your stirrup, your skirts flying, that
You had taken an oath to your three sisters that you would not
Give any gallant more than one kiss before a proper betrothal,
And that they had taken the same oath before a medallion
Blessed by the likeness of St. Adelaide. With modesty, you
Said that you wanted no other and that nightingales would

Become marsh frogs before you let another gallant carry
Your colors and that though I was an imperial *ministeriale,*
One day I would come into a fief of my own and you knew
You could wear down your father regarding the bad match
He was eyeing for you with that old buzzard out of Mainz.
As we rode out of that dear place, the wind making our reins
And sleeve tips dance a jolly jig, I was sure that, in spite of
St. Adelaide's peruse, I might steal another kiss or two from you
Beneath those beeches or some hill bedecked with pretty lindens.

Alas, your father, turned Guelph, took you with him to Italy,
To fight in defense of the Pope against the Kaiser of Rome.
I never saw you again-but many times I have ridden my horse
Past that stand of trees, that grove, and remembered the kiss with
Longing, remembered the flowers raining down without end.

LIME

Tension leaves the warrior's hand
As he catches the lime's green shine
In the rain beading the point of the
Practice sword

SAKE

Balm for the palms bruised by the bokken
The brush of the crane's moon-dusted wing
Held and holding the cobalt blue of the
Sake flask

CHEVRON STATION

Morning fog burn

Black man on a bicycle
His handlebar basket brimming with lemons
Sweater the color of old celery
Circles the pumps preaching that
He will overcome America and he will
Sit down at the right hand of
Jesus

MEDIEVAL GERMAN MINNESONG

In these days, bitter as the berries of the mountain ash,
When the ministers of conflict go about the land like a
Bunch of Franconian boors blowing into their *dudelsacks*,
And the poor and needy, tired of the boot and the spur,
Weary of the sword, flail and the torch, cry to God for relief,
In voices piercing as the summer hawks-I remind myself that
God *is* just and that in His own good time, He will punish
And root out the Lover of Blood and The Bad Counselor,
As a young knight, clips away the thorns from the
Golden rose of *amour*, and gifts it to a maiden
Matchless as the morning pearls. Emperors and kings
Who publish crushing fiats and decrees, will not go on
Forever, caparisoned in gold and silver-they will face an
Upright decision when their souls are required at
The Tribunal of Truth. None will escape the fire of
That verdict, they will wail like the Ninevites before
The words of the prophet Nahum. There is an end to
The lance and the destrier-to the shield face shellacked
In the crimson of autumn maples. I am old and tired of war.
If I were called, I could not sit a horse caparisoned for battle;
My hands are cramped-fingers crooked as the crabs foraging
On the shores of Italy or Sicily. My sword sleeps in its
Scabbard of red leather with gilded rams' heads: it is as an
Old monk dozing in a monastery's garden, head bowed down
By draughts of April's bee-mead breezes. The small green
Locusts weave in and out of my scarlet mantle's folds.

Sitting on a stone at the edge of a stream in the woods,
I watched the water strive against stone, the smash of
Light-stippled current and foam against rock and thought
How God grinds down and smooths the kingdoms of Man
With time and calamity-reduces them like these pebbles of green,
Red, orange and blue. Shifting now and then, because I
Am always pained and chafed by the wounds of my youth,
Gained in Italy for the Holy *Kaiser*, I listened to the voice of
The waters and joined my soul to The Master as the chausses
Of the flower's dust befits the bee's leg, closing my eyes
To take in the viols, lutes and tambours of the little ones
Overhead, the trills, chirps and songs of the high consortiums
Of the *Kleine Reich* of green and gold that surrounds us all.

Blind, I caught the crunch of leaf and twig beneath the
Little hooves of doe and fawn; the muttered thunder of an
Old boar, well away, on the other side of the stream,
Beyond the beam-shot barbicans of beech and oak.
Here, in the wood's cool, I could believe in a world at peace:
I could hear the step of the Lamb, and imagine this stream
Was but a reflection of the Jordan in distant Outremer.
My soul found its salve in the shine and shadow playing
Across the green spears of the lime's leaves-advancing
And retreating with the wind's fragrant breath-it is easy to
Make a world here.

I opened my eyes to watch the lime flowers light down,
Bright yellow and white, swept along and sucked down by
The moil and thrash of the turbulent waters and was minded
Of the arms, shields and pennons of comrades fallen from
Sickeness in the Romfahrt over the alps, or wasted in the
Wars against the Pope's Guelphs. I saw them clearly in the
Ephemeral flowers tossed and drowned, mashed against the
Rock's harsh mail-roses and flowerets fair as the blossoms
Of the tree that grew through the roof of the Volsungs' hall.
Here, I see the green hunter's horn on white of *junge* Heinz,
Unblemished as a young foal, swept off the siege-ladder in

     TODD FRENCH

Milan by the cruel oil, his flesh and mail blackened as the
Olives in Outremer. Ah, another petal falls from the lime,
Dragged down beneath the turgid foam and I can make out
The red double battle axes on blue of Peter von Palermo,
That Swabian-Norman *gasmule*, strong as a Theban bull,
Blessed with the voice of a linnet, red-haired with the wide
Laughing mouth, who perished in Sicily from the poisoned
Tips of Saracen arrows? Who knocked over more papal knights
Than he when his destrier was between his thighs? Ah, see, see,
Another flower is born along-I see the three black mullets on
Gold of Wolfram der Erste, who was always first to fly to
A breach like a young eagle bearing prey to his eyrie; that
Thuringian bore his battleax as a *Spruch-Sprecher* a pure
Judgment-the hooves of his steed crushed the helms of
Lombards like the north wind stamps the roses of the bower
Flat. What an ill day when he fell at Cortenuova-slain by the
Guelph trash! How open-handed he was when it was time
For the sharing of bread in the hard times!

Where are the great knights of my youth-the flower of the
German lands that went forth to do mighty deeds, tossing
Their heads like the mountain harts, the sun flashing from
Their helms and crests like dawn's pheons striking the tines
Of the great stags? Were they a dream-nothing but a whisp
Of the mind's mist that disappears when the lark calls one
From sleep? The stream whips the lime tree's treasures along,
One after another as they drift down, like *pfennigs* flung from
The purses of fat bishops to the commoners-falling in lovely
Spirals, gilded for a moment like the failing virtue of the
Daystar's armies when they were suborned to go up against
God in the renegade's mail. How can I not see them in their
Former glory-burning like brands for glory as they sat their
Saddles beneath the eeling of the imperial eagles-the crimson
And mauve of sunset making them flash like the stews of Mount
Etna's slopes. Their voices scrape at the inside of my skull like a
Small wind whistling through thistle and burdock-I imagine I
Can hear all their ghosts-their tongues low lyres competing with

The ragged flap of campaign tents. What happened to the oaths
They swore when we crossed the alps-what happened to the
Chaste maids they left behind-who gifted them with braids and
Locks of their dark or wheaten tresses, coiled in pouches, scrips,
Woven into the rings from which the bright swords jingled?
I remember the sweet music of their reins and the shields that
Tolled like bells against the saddle horns and rang like tambours
Against the mail-clad shoulder.

The times are bad now, and there is little justice to be had.
Everyone-the *graf*, the *ministeriale*, the churchman and scholar
Practices oppression-the knight puts on serge and waits by the
Roadside for the small folk with their cart, for the sojourner,
The pilgrim with the flowering staff come from Jerusalem or
The north heaths, to take a spoil and a prey. Bandits meet at
Night like the river wolves-and the judges, ah, *the judges*,
They take a bribe and fill their saddlebags with blood money,
And the peasant and the upright groans like the bears come
Out of their winter dens. The princes strive with the kaiser,
And the kaiser with the princes, like dogs and crows over a
Dead roan-and tumult follows tumult follows tumult and
Nothing settles. I sit here, next to the stream, marking how
The rushing water smooths the rocks, grinds the bottom
Stones against one another, reduces them to tiny glints and sharps.
Perhaps there is solace in that even if the linden and beech
Blossoms must fall and drown-be whirled away into murk,

Like worldly valor, youth, nobility and courage, so in time,
Time the ax and maul of the Master, will in time, smash and
Smooth the castles and plans of the great and the cruel. The
Great waters go on, the stones wear down, and the green trees
Flower in spring and the blossoms pass, ah, the blossoms of
Youth and vigor pass as in a dream, bright as the gleanings
Of summer's mulberries.

I am an old man, tired of the ways of war, weary of lawlessness.
May the Lord return and His kingdom be an everlasting one!

   Todd French

THE SECRET SERVICE AGENT'S NIGHTMARE

It is the same each night: he is lashed to a gurney, his
Right forearm bound with tacky rust-red dressing, and
He is borne-without human hand-through white enamel
Hospital corridors, overhead fluorescents reduced to flickering
Green foxfire-witch-wink of undersea lantern fish. And all about,
German shepherds pacing, running, jumping, clawing and jawing
At the sides of his conveyance like a cut-rate chthonic guard
Courtesy of Anubis, delivering him to the dog-headed man's
Funeral barge. Snapping muzzles-multitudinous as furry organ pipes
Bunch around the steel rails protecting his arms-Scylla's
Barking girdle stoked to max-black gums shiny as fresh
Hot top, freshets of drool splashing across his blankets
And restraints, wet yellow incisors tearing at the bars and
Flailing bedclothes. He can barely raise his head to glimpse the
New wound badly bandaged, belling anguish like a foghorn,
Even as his dream-trammeled synapses, hyper-aware and shrilling
Like white bellbirds or sun conures, instantly make the
Connection that the old one, sustained on the right thigh,
Gotten when the hound, without any warning suddenly snapped
Snapped its leash in the Rose Garden and leapt for him-has yet to heal.
Bound and unable to scream, he is shuttled forward every faster,
Then rounding corner after corner as the walls turn to cave stone,
Picked out by the crimson flicker of old timber's road-flare light,
Scribed with atavistic drawings of dire wolves and mangled
Stick figures, all the while the air grows contrails of blood's
Auto yard spice, squamous, humid with wet fur, piss-trickle,
Old meat and marrow, the smell of impending violence as

Over the castanet-click of snapping fangs, snarls and barks

A cold voice intones, reasonably, from his agent's popped earbud
Lying next to his head:

"This is The President's Dog. He cannot be put down."
"This is The President's Dog. He cannot be put down."
"This is The President's Dog. He cannot be put down."
"This is The President's Dog. He cannot be put down."

BORDERS/CHERRY BLOSSOMS

Maybe God is gifting America with an Adrianople debacle,
A collapse of Roman horses before the small pony men with
Slashed cheeks and mouse-skin cloaks flood across our
Broken borders, driving ragged phalanxes of wheat-haired
Goths before them. Perhaps, this is the time, in the Spring
Of Rehoboam (who lost the undivided kingdom of Israel),
That it all comes apart; when our own senile Rehoboam,
Cursing half the country to perdition, is guided by God
To take away safety and security, to put our sons and
Daughters at risk, because we are far from Him, we are far.
It is possible that as the murex-purple cope of Valens
Was trodden into the mire by the haggard Greutungs
And Alans, they, tired of bartering boys and girls for
Dog-flesh, tired of paying in kin for moldy refugee fare,
That we will see the same in our lifetime. Following
His State of the Union address, the President recanted
Referring to the illegal immigrant who murdered a
Young girl as "illegal" because according to his critics
No One is Illegal and it all seems mad as a mad meadow
Scramble of sightless rabbits spreading myxomatosis.

Straw-heads hold us in our hands.

And yet I am thinking of cherry blossoms.

And yet, I am thinking of the cherry blossoms over at
Huntington Beach Central Park-the trees a gift of fifty

Some years from Huntington Beach's sister city of Anjo,
In Japan. The Cherry Blossom Festival (Hanami) this year
Will be March 20th to April 14th. Anjo is in southern Aichi
Prefecture, some 19 miles from the city of Nagoya; and
Proceeds go to a youth exchange between the two cities.
The event is down the block as it were, and it makes me '
Smile-because here is amity, goodwill, cultural exchange
Defined in snowdrifts, spirals, conger eel-shimmies of
Pink and white blossoms breathed out in Roman candle
Candescence amidst the sun-daubed green of the showing
Grove. I am imagining the crowds, (diverse and) appreciative
Of Asia's culture, winding around the vendor tents,
Passing over items in the pop-ups, spirits humming with the
Light-wafted bliss of Biwa and Shakuhachi notes from
Each blossom and bud.

I am thinking of the long-bodied white and blue herons
Ghosting down in the marsh waters behind the bandstand,
Beautiful as brush-kiss of sable calligraphy strokes on
Rice paper-I can see bird rendered with brevity of lines,
Blending into bank and tree-bone, a deft splotch of red
Sun behind brink of water pleat, with a black ladder of
Kanji in the corner of the sheet.

I can see, when the festival goes into night, the quick
Limn of marsh bird, hawk and owl wing splitting the
Rut-bound of the March moon's rabbit shadow, and imagine
The crowds gathered before the trees, bark stamped
With fatigue patches of silver and jet, blossoms
Falling in their gentle rataplan, caught in coldfire,
Speckling clothes, faces, hair-thin skim of Sakura
Snow casting its mizzle on dog muzzle and stroller's
Hood. How can you not find *peace*, feel at *peace*,
Watching the pale, twisting skeins of petals pure as
A nun's wind-blown coif. Watching the undulance of
Branch and limb-wood tines trying to clutch the roll from
Tree bole of chime, string-shiver from hirsute leaf,

Who couldn't feel the soul lift like a crane, spring into
Space like a small frog from a moon-frizzed cattail's
Head? Joy jams within like a *taiko* percussion group.
Here is friendship's pale sigils: rooted firmly in the earth,
Bestowing the benefice of God's crafting-hand
(do cherry blossoms fall at five centimeters per second?),
In the freefall of the fair and ephemeral things of this
Fading world.

Straw-heads hold us in their hands-hollow men,
Hollow as an old bottle gourd.

And yet I am thinking of cherry blossoms.

In spite of the bitter memories of war, there is goodwill
Between the cities of Huntington Beach and Anjo.

Maybe we are looking at an Adrianople debacle,
A God-given collapse of Roman horses and the
Small pony men with slashed cheeks and mouse-skin
Cloaks driving beaten wheat-haired Goths and Alans
Before them are on the way and our feelings matter
No more than an almoner of whelk and turban shells,
Hair on a dust mite but whether this from God or no,
The chaos and abrogation of a constitutional duty,
Nothing we can reverse. It is possible that *this is it*.
Still, I am dreaming of spring's advent, the first brush
Of its solar kiss-like a youth skimming a new growth of
Beard against the cheek of his girlfriend, making her blush,
Sending her cinnamon braids dancing. Yes, I am looking
Forward to the detonation of bud and bloom, the fragrant
Breakers of pink and white rushing across green grass,
Spotting the eyelids of the baby in the stroller, catching
The edge of a hand, an older man's spike of beard, while
Rufous and Anna's hummingbirds speed from tree to tree,
As if to say: "Here, here! Check it out! Don't lag behind!"
And phoebe and sparrow, bee and butterfly not behind.
You can imagine walking through the grove, thoughts

Producing their own rice-paper and black *kanji* strokes
Each second-a green finch lifting from a blossom-heavy
Branch, a grinning toddler reaching up to snatch a snowflake
Fall of petal, a corgi or Irish setter jumping up to gulp down
A couple of blooms while you compose the haikus and tankas born
Of flower and light, of warmth and wellbeing. It isn't hard to
Imagine the pleasure of the Birth Season's bounty-of setting
Yourself beneath a tree and, closing your eyes, imagine
Wind's whisper through green bamboo, the *clop-clop* of
Fountain patter, arc of scarlet bridge and mini-donjon.
It isn't hard to imagine the weave of lounging kimono,
The tickling perfume of cherry blossom, yellow
Chrysanthemum, red rose, purple wisteria and camelia.
It isn't hard to close your eyes and send the mind skipping
Like a young hare in buckwheat and say:

I am thinking of the cherry blossoms.

I am thinking of our generous friends from Anjo.

I am thinking of spring.

NEITHER TAKEN OR GIVEN

Matthew 22:30
New International Version

[30] At the resurrection people will neither marry nor be given in marriage; they will be
like the angels in heaven.

In heaven, your wife will no longer be your wife, and who knows,
In what gold or cyanine precinct of the divine realm she will serve,
Because, amidst the overwhelming joy and love of being in the Kingdom,
God will have good work for the two of you to do-whatever it might be.
Men and women will no longer be taken or given in marriage, as the
Gospel proclaims, but they will live as the angels. The human mind and soul
Cannot grasp such a divorce: history and intimacy reduced to pueblo potsherds,
To a swan's wing-skim of memory (the former things), the union in disunion,
The kisses un-kissed, the bed of joining broken down into IKEA pieces,
The starry gazes of youth's courtship un-starred-but the *friendship*, the *friendship*
Deeper now (with everyone/resurrected/God/seraphim/cherubim), infinite in
Understanding and the higher affections-will remain. It balks, the brain,
Grasping the Idea of The Beloved disappearing like a fog's mica shine from
Tree and vehicle when morning's light arrives-the marriage contract
Unwinding like a nightingale's plaintive airs (where is she where is the one)
Before a northeaster takes it away, whips it away. No one knows how to
Translate the human here-and-now (the current love) into the aerialist ease
And please of angelease-the endless symphony of goldshine's notes of praise
And service-exultation without end. When you are lifted into the sweet
Atmospheric river of *hosannas, blessed bes, honor and glories,* when you
Are in the presence of the triune Godhead basking in joy everlasting you

Won't cry out for the Helpmate and she won't cry out for you because of
The wonder of What Is/purity of Spirit humming like an electric eel's discharge
Through perfected flesh-*what will you yearn for what will you yearn for*
When you are in the presence of The Ancient One of Days-will you weep for
The ring/the kiss/the parted veil her veil/her smile/her eyes catching the
Butter glaze and kindle of Churchlight when you stand in the holy realm
Where the plectrums stroke worship's fire from the lyre, kinnor, harp
In The Father's House the God-designed city paradise the better country

I don't think so.

Even as you are taking baby-steps on the streets of transparent gold

You will remember (though neither taken or given), you will remember

As Isaac recalls day's end when he was in the wheaten fields and looked up to see
The Intended, Rebekkah, lighting down from her colt to run to him.

The former love.
The old love.
The old fire.
The bitterness of Goldenseal and sweetness of cinnamon.
The love that made a family (or not).

Wherever the two of you are in the new heavens

How could you forget her or she you?

AFTER THE WINDS ARE DONE

After the winds are done, the street is full of the rich brown
Detritus of old palm fronds-like shaggy patches of shrugged-off
Bison hide or a Pandemic dump of small, dead dachshunds.
And even now that the worst is over, the wind whispers
Insistently amidst the green pleats and the petal-stripped
Prunus trees in its nasty sibilant way:

"We're just taking a break. Be prepared."

ALLEN'S HUMMINGBIRD

When I was in the backyard, practicing my bokken strikes,
Enjoying how the winds had sent the white flotillas of
Cumulus scattering across the sky's cerulean blue,
An Allen's hummingbird with its bib of orange-red fire
Tucked about its throat lit down on the branch of my
Neighbor's guava tree, cocked its little head, zipped away
And then returned to its same perch and looked down at me

As if to say:

Don't mind me, I'm just checking your form.

I lowered my sword and laughed, thinking:

Who am I to be so serious about myself!

SUNFLOWERS

Of the eleven or twelve giant sunflowers that have sprouted
In the planter against the backyard wall-only one has flowered, its
Leonine head, above all the other droopy green periscopes,
Opened wide like the eye of an apostle in some alternate night in
Gethsemane, who managed to stay half-awake to keep a look-out
for the torches of traitors and temple guards.

I WOULD BARTER MANY A BRIGHT AND BLAZING STAR

I would barter many a bright and blazing star,
If heaven gave me access to that almonry,
To see that matchless maiden, coming from afar,
Shining like solar pheons spread upon the sea.
When she draws near, I tremble like a barley wand
In the clasp of an Easter breeze. Let me affirm:
Since God designed the fair and female Eidolon,
No mother breached and brought a better girl to term.

Oh, she is fair: as pallid as a paschal lamb,
In grace, becalmed, no spirit made for wuthering;
In form and measure, she is peerless, crown to jambe,
Her flowing tresses blacker than a grackle's wing.

I am a rough knight, little known for bard's disport:
E'en so, I have seen her once or twice at court.

     TODD FRENCH

TRUE LOVE/LUKE 5:18-25

The hands flurrying at the roof tiles and roof grass,
Casting them aside like a fox vixen digging out a kits' burrow
Or a badger working on a set-sobs wracking their chests,
Tears leaking from the corner of the eyes as the hole forms,
And widens-widens-even as the tips of their fingers bruise
And bleed-they can't stop! There's a fraction of uplifted arm
In garment weave caught in the growing aperture and day's
Pixilated, thick, streaming beams-chests ratcheting with the
Effort-the tremors going through the limbs with the realization
That *we can do this-we can do this*-the furnace of small hope
Growing, expanding like the scintillant afterbirth of a star,
The hands-their hands- clawing away more sun-warmed tiles
And the breach growing that there's The Teacher's shoulder,
The afternoon flints sewn in his locks glinting from his shoulder.
Someone secures the ropes to the pallet.

One or another of them-the workers, the friends-darts a brief
Glance at the man on the pallet, leaning on his elbows,
Tears coursing down *his* cheeks at the profundity and
Commitment of feeling that defies the moment, deafens the
Growing sea-throttle of pebble and comber coming from the
Uptilted faces below, thick as rows of lentils or corn stalks,
Awe scribed on their brows like the wind-cuts in the Hebron Hills,
Each of them trying to reclaim their scattered thoughts:
To have friends that love you so-to not give up on you!
Would someone do that for me-drag my bones up to the roof?
Had they not stood there, bemused, stolid as tent pegs,

When the first bounded up the ladder, followed by others,
And then the man on the sleeping mat hauled heavenward
Like a kinnor's Song of Ascent and they, the outer ring
Waiting for balm and healing, waiting their turn-what were
They thinking-or had cogent thought become scattered as
As wind-tossed thistle-swung up from day's quotidian dust
Like mini cyclones of chaff on the threshing-room floor?

What bloomed in their hearts-like the cotton thistle's
Purple petals nestled within the green ring of spikes,

*Look at the love look at the love they have for this man
Ah God let The Teacher accept him please The Teacher heal!*

Surely, the entreaties flew from their hearts as they looked up,
Their agues, fevers, discharges, cataracts, foreshortened limbs
Forgotten as they watched the man's friends ripped the roof off,
Charitable as those birds, the Arabian babblers who will
Squabble amongst themselves to help another build its nest
Or feed its babies.

And the man on the pallet weeping, shoulders bunching
With sobs, to himself, scanning the sweat-sheened faces
Of his friends his friends oh God his friends as the roof
Parts enough for the glimpse of The Man The Man his face
Pointing upwards now, his compassion, his love capable of
Shearing off the house-top his eyes his eyes his light
His light coming up to meet him reaching upwards
Mercy high as the arms of the Mount Tabor oaks

And as they lowered him

Did the man on the pallet with the lame legs look
At his friends and say to himself, shaking with the
Enormity of the emotion hat rendered emotion moot

*My God, my God, that you would do this for me,
My God, my God, that you would!*

　　　　　　　Todd French

THE MEADISH BEES HAVE COME TO PAY THEIR OBSEQUIES

The meadish bees have come to pay their obsequies,
To buzz and bumble 'bout her sleevelet's rumpled burl,
Around her circlet where the flowers tide and twirl,
Like summer waves up-raging in their surgencies.
Ah, my God, extend this moment, I pray you, please:
To lie here on this high hill, holding the best girl
In Christendom-her cinnamon braids undone, unfurled,
Her beech-green eyes a-spark with sweet felicities.

It is good to lie here now, trading kiss for kiss,
Beneath the blue, while heaven's crenellations drift,
Shredding and sledding, while the sylphs, their powers shift:
For such things, our hearts, like skylarks, sing their bliss.
Let the sun hang as it did on Joshua's Day,
Fixed while I hold her: finest Lady, dearest may.

TELL YOUR WIFE OR GIRLFRIEND

Tell your wife or girlfriend she is the aureate light,
That the day of her birth was a confluence of beams,
A conspiracy of graces brought together by God.
Say to her, with eye focused as an American kestrel's,
Gratitude vast as the pleated skin of the green Aegean,
That when He spoke her soul's lucents into life,
There in the comforts of her blessed mother's womb
Your far from equidistant heart, not knowing her,
Not knowing her, nonetheless went nova, went off like
All the fireworks on a Lincolnshire festival eve,
Cranked itself into one long summer fair
Calliope cry which did not stop wailing,
Happy klaxon that it was, until the day you met her.

Take her hand in yours and tell her:
That was when the scattered tongues of roses
And chrysanthemums, love's *lingua franca*,
Delicate as the feathered antennae of the
Actias Isabellae moth

Made sense.

LIFE LESSONS

(DAMIAN LECHOSZEST'S PAINTING)

There is something so beautiful, so spartan, so entrancing
Regarding the masterful twinning of generations and hard work
Contained within the unfussy canvas of Polish artist
Damian Lechoszest's painting in which three women,
Two young, the other old, go about the business of
Plucking goose feathers. The tableau bespeaks a particular
Mystery that goes beyond the miracle of tinctures and brush.
It's a bit of Old World Magic that's in play here. Check out
The Breugelian earthiness about the room, the bare boards
Beneath the trio's feet-the gray, the stolid stone wall and table
That serves as a backdrop-the well-used black kettle
And the fox-fur hue of a propped-up cutting board;
The stingy splash of sunlight on the wall to the right.
And yet in spite of the tight confines of the plucking chamber
(and these geese seem resigned and well-acclimated to
The wearisome biz of having their feathers removed
Handful by handful) that there is something just wonderful,
And mystifying that draws the admiring eye-as if you had gone
Into the ruins of an old machine-shop and found a
Single blue iris growing from out of a spider-web
Of wall cracks: a taper of glacial blue glowing amidst
Galaxies of dust mites suspended in streaming shafts of
Dirty light

Or while hiking through an autumn forest, spellbound by
Nature's gold and russet livery-stopping in your tracks

When you see a gold heart medallion, broken in half and
Nailed to the tree's rough skin.

Why are you smiling, young girl?

Why are you smiling, beautiful girl?

What is the old lady saying to win that smile?

Here are the two young women on their plucking stools,
In their short white shifts-the girl in the middle's legs splayed
Before her feather receptacle-the base of their smooth bosoms
Visible, reddish brown braids resting against their chests,
Faces colored with the patina of exertion's honest sweat-a few
Wayward strands of hair hanging down from the brow of the girl on the
Left who is intent on the work-half-listening it seems, to the
Old woman on the far right. Our gaze is drawn to the white of
The shifts, the white of the geese, the pulls of feather like
Cotton fibers heaped in the containers. We take in the flush
On the faces, the bound ropes of smooth, shiny hair,
The sensuality of bare legs and feet, the orange of the goose bills;
All of this bespeak life, life, beauty constrained and free, within
The simple capture of the bucolic plucking-chamber's stripped,
Chilly mien. You can feel the cold of stone stinging foot soles.
And, ah, these geese, these geese: nothing surly about them;
These birds endure the removal of their feathers with the aplomb of
Martyrs being shaved for an Inquisition's show-trial. Well, come on:
Better the plucking-pot than the cooking pot, right? And the girls
In their white shifts: is this painting a metaphor for the plucking
Of other things for maidens come of marriage age?

And here is the mystery: the middle girl with the splayed legs,
Head turned to listen to the old lady on her right, the latter
Dressed in her earthen garb and white apron and bonnet,
Peasant's face staring off into space, her left hand raised,
Index finger pointing upward, bowl on her lap and feathers
Clumps filling her fisted right hand. She is speaking to the
Duo and while the girl on the left concentrates on the task

At hand, the girl in the middle has turned her head to the
Older woman, and her lips are quirked in a slight, impish smile
As she listens, not pausing from the work, her left hand
Just grazing the goose's neck. Something the old lady has said
Has surprised this one bit of human jollity as women pare birds
Down to their small feathers-there is an enigma here.

Why are you smiling?

Why are you smiling, beautiful girl?

There is the moment of the soul's candescence in the
Dreary chamber, with its metal tubs, dark metal cauldron,
Brasen jugs, metal feather bowls heightened by the glow
Of skin, white of shift, bareness of leg-*why are you smiling?*

Is the old woman yours and the other girl's grandmother or are
None of you related and what is she going on about?
Trued and tried aphorisms, proverbs and platitudes about
Country life-or a long-vanished youth in which she went
About the plucking of men's heartstrings as easy as pulling out
Hanks of goose-down? Is she informing these maidens
About what's good for the goose and gander when it comes to
Amours or is she recalling the loving ministrations of a
Long-dead husband or a lover who went to war, how they
Laid sprays of lavender or chaplets of bluebells by her
Night table in the morning while she was asleep, just as the
Morning's light spilled across your coverlet? Is she
Telling them how her father would take her on horseback
Rides as a little girl, sitting in front of him as they
Clopped along one of the local roads at sunset, dying day-fire
Red as campfire coals leaking through the strangling intertwined
Branches and limbs of a tree tunnel and how she caught the

Distant scent of honeysuckle and jasmine-the smell of sweat
And mead on your father's clothes, the scraps of song from a
Wren and the relentless hammer of a woodpecker? Is she passing on
An admonition about marrying too early or too young?

A fine piece of art tells a story, leaves you with a mystery that
You will never solve but works on your mind with the stubbornness
Of a deathwatch beetle tapping away in a wall-the lingering fade-out
Of the contrail of a rocket jettisoning a stage as it blasts across a
Star-lush length of winter sky.

I look at the girl on the middle stool with her head turned, lips
In a slight smile.

Why are you smiling?

Why are you smiling, beautiful girl?

Who or what has won that light from you?

TODD FRENCH

TELL YOUR WIFE OR GIRLFRIEND

Tell her that her eyes are brighter than the Seine
In June, or the candescent traceries and flairs of
Bengal light-do not hold back, for we are on the cusp
Of a Life in Wartime, and shall we prate in sweetness
Like the mellifluous wits of old Toulouse and Quercy,
On another day-another eve, while this world's northeasters
Swell their stormy fronts like fat burghers' bellies?
You don't need a houppelande and liripipe for garb,
Flutes, vielles or psalteries borrowed or begged
From Messers Betran, Guillem, Francois or Pierre, a full
Moon red as velum, a hurdy-gurdy of crickets
And nightjars to lend the night gravis to express
Your feelings for her. You do not have to be a
Medieval French troubadour singing her merits from
Castle to castle, a blanket of flagstones for your troubles.
If this is the world's long autumn, let us make good
Use of our time while the sun's rowel pricks us to laughter.

Attend what I say: I am no starveling loafing
At some county's court, singing for fat chops and
The waft of wine's vermillion-I am just an old man,
Living in sunny Southern Cal, and the guerdons of
Word-loft are not for me-neither are the green laurels
Made for brow-binding. I am no troubadour competing
With others for a warm corer-launching words like whippets
Bound for hound-coursing. It's just me: an old duffer used
To troubling people with my words for I sleep less than

I did in my youth-and The Muse is a wolf making
Glissandos at odd hours, now and then dropping a
Rose at my feet. But as I was saying: we are on
The cusp of a Life in Wartime, and the thunderheads
Of this world's northeasters are grunting and booming
Like fat burgers' bellies or tuskers belching as they
Look for the deep truffles. Do not, I say, not keep declarations
Of love to yourself like silver in an almoner's sack.

If she be in your arms on the couch while you are
Watching old episodes of House on Netflix, a bowl of
Popcorn shared between you, or you are both folding laundry
In the kitchen-take a moment to lean over and tell her
How much you love and appreciate her-whether she be
Your wife of longstanding, or a maid in the first months of
Infatuation and knowledge: If you are holding hands
In the wood-lanes at sunset, when the birds dirge
For the last lags of scarlet and tangelo painted on the pines,
Before the cold winds climb and the gray clouds hide
The sun's *Or* and vermillion-let her know your heart.
I'm not telling you to prate like the mellifluous wits of
Toulouse and Quercy-to spill your guts in the lingua of
Long-dead Languedoc-it's not for me to tell you to
Sing her fair in Huntington beach, Costa Mesa, Irvine,
Or Aliso Viejo-or far as Santa Barbara or Monterey.
That's for those knights of the lyre from Old France.

Reach for her hand at the kitchen table after finishing
The bills-give her a kiss on the cheek when the last
Of the groceries are put away, the bags folded and stowed
Above the dryer. Take her in your arms and inhale the
Fragrance of honeysuckle/clean creek water after she
Has plucked the latest batch of dandelions from the
Front lawn. We do not need to be possessed by the
Blood's bright vermillion, our arms burdened with
A bevy of flutes, vielles and psalteries-trying to gust
A good ballade or sirventes like Messers Betran, Guillem,

     TODD FRENCH

Francois or Pierre-they had their moment in the sun!
Be she a wife of longstanding or a maid in the first months
Of infatuation and knowledge-she deserves to hear the
Confession of your heart. More than ever, the nation
Is on the cusp of Life in Wartime and with war
Comes the death of mellifluous wits whatever the season.

Should she be the girlfriend of no more than a month or two,
Maybe the words will come easier, as well as the kisses,
Sweet as the summer lingua of long-dead Languedoc,
Dear as the music coaxed from the flutes, vielles and psalteries
Stowed in the beaks and tongues of jays, nightingales and
Warblers. When you are young, it is easy to get carried away
By New Love's luminaries of gold and vermillion and to
Prate like those old wits with their lyres from Toulouse and
Quercy-but we are heading bit by bit toward a Life lived
In Wartime-and no one should take these days for granted.
Some bad dreams-dreamt for us by nations-have taken off
Like whippets wound-up for hound-coursing and who can say

When we will saunter amidst the olive groves of Peace?
There are nightmares to be bought by the guerdons of
The fretful sub-conscious-even an old duffer like me can
See the writing on the wall. Frame the plain-speak of Cherish,
When you hold her in the circle of your arms.
It is easy to be reticent about the things we should say,
When we are old and the shine has worn off the full moon's
Red velum-and our ears are half-deaf to the hurdy-gurdy
Of summer's crickets and nightjars-and age creates thought gaps,
Mind-spindle's fray-and our days are wearying as we grapple
With imperatives of guerdons, savings flat as an almoner's sack
Following the ebb of mendicants and beggars from the church steps.
It is too easy to forget the expressions of the heart's vermillion,
To settle into our cares like hiding under a blanket of flagstones,
Forgetting how the sun's rowel pricked us to laughter, in the
First blush of Felicity's works-deft as the hart chasing the doe.
I am an old duffer, but I recognize that though the Muse is a wolf

Making glissandos-pushing me pen-wise-I must do the best
To recover the roses she drops at my feet and to proffer them
To The One that I love. There is no help in life's autumn
From Messers Bertan, Guillem, Francois and Pierre,
And who knows when the flutes, vielles or psalteries will return
When we are living a Life in the sanguine hours of Wartime?

CONCLUSION

Tell her that her eyes are brighter than the Seine
In June, or the candescent traceries and flairs of
Bengal light- do not hold back, for we are on the cusp
Of a Life in Wartime. Shall we prate in sweetness
Like the mellifluous wits of Toulouse and Quercy,
On some other day or eve, while this world's northeasters
Go swelling their cloudy fronts like the bellies of fat burghers?

***Messers Bertran, Guillem, Francois and Pierre refer to
Medieval French troubadours

HOMELESS

1 Samuel 29:3-5
New English Translation

[3] The leaders of the Philistines asked, "What about these Hebrews?" Achish said to the leaders of the Philistines, "Isn't this David, the servant of King Saul of Israel, who has been with me for quite some time?[a] I have found no fault with him from the day of his defection until the present time!"[b]

[4] But the leaders of the Philistines became angry with him and said[c] to him, "Send the man back! Let him return to the place that you assigned him! Don't let him go down with us into the battle, for he might become[d] our adversary in the battle. What better way to please his lord than with the heads of these men?[e] [5] Isn't this David, of whom they sang as they danced,[f]
'Saul has struck down his thousands,
but David his tens of thousands'?"

Imagine David and his troops getting up before first light, before the
Philistine camp came alive with the clatter of horse-neigh, pan fry and
Armor buckle-troops yawning and complaining about getting the
Graveyard hours of army guard duties two days in a row. You can imagine
The young David and his Hebrews-ghosts gobbed up in the helm slits
Of the hostile Philistines, non-entities now, not allies-rolling up their own
Armor, tying their packs on to their steeds even as the first streamers of
The desert's tangelo light strikes the canvas and finial of the soldiers
Dreaming awake of unseaming King Saul and his sons in the spear-scuffle.
Did the future King of Israel, himself a shepherd, reflect on how he was
Being driven out of camp as if he and his young men were diseased ewes

Suffering tetanus or pox, culled out of the herd of the uncircumcised?
I wonder if, as brought up in the enemy council, if a couple of Philistines
Didn't spring up from their morning rashers of bacon and shout:
"Saul, Saul, has slain his ten thousands, but David, David, slain his
Ten thousands!" Were there jeers and snickers? And did David recall,
As he began the task of leading his men back to fire-smote Ziklag,
To further abandonment-all the wives and girls stolen by the war-reduced
Amalekites like the women of Shiloh by the near-extinct Benjaminites,
That it was an irony the Philistines remembered what he had forgotten:
The boy with the slingshot who had dropped the mountain of gold greaves
And breastplate with one shot-sent the giant's shield-bearer skittering
For the foe-host's lines like a sand cat for its burrow, the guy shouting
Dagon oh Dagon he did it he diditdiditdiditdiditwithastoneastoneastone!

I forgot who I was. I forgot who I was supposed to be.

As he and his retainers decamped, Saul ahead wanting to make a wall-ornament of
Him, and the enemy who rejected him, his myth, his desperado valor, how did
He summon up the kinnor-strings of his harpist's heart to reassure the soldiers whose
Hopes and expectations followed him like the dust-moil of a locust swarm?
What could he play for them in The Key of Faith as the morning bowl of sky
Filled in with strands of beaten platinum and rose?

What did soul say to soul:

I am as the worker bee banished from the honeycombs of Hebron.

I am as the worker bee rejected by the honeycombs of Gath.

I can do nothing but buzz on a square of air-where do I light?

My Lord and God, where is my home, where do I go?

UNRIPE FIGS

In sunset's wash of bronze light
Balanced on the fig tree's branches
Telling each other no no they're not ripe yet
A sparrow a warbler and afraid to say a word
In case he might offend the other two

A hummingbird